Also by Ed DeVos

The Stain
The Chaplain's Cross
Revenge at Kings Mountain

FAMILY
of
WARRIORS

FAMILY

of

WARRIORS

ED DEVOS

Deeds Publishing | Athens

Published by Deeds Publishing in Athens, GA
www. deedspublishing. com

Printed in The United States of America

Cover design by Mark Babcock
Text layout by Matt King

Illustrations by Gary Marathon

Library of Congress Cataloging-in-Publications data is available upon request.

ISBN 978-1-944193-88-1
EISBN 978-1-944193-89-8

Books are available in quantity for promotional or premium use. For information, email info@deedspublishing. com.

First Edition, 2017

10 9 8 7 6 5 4 3 2 1

To all who have served our country. To all who are serving our country. And to all who will serve our country.

CONTENTS

Maps

ACKNOWLEDGEMENTS

THE SEEDS FOR WRITING THIS BOOK WERE PLANTED WHEN, AS A SMALL boy, I watched my father put on the uniform of the United States Air Force. Then, later, as I put on the uniform of the United States Army, I was privileged to serve around many men who exhibited valor and courage, honor and integrity on a daily basis. It was those men, both of higher and lower rank than me, who provided the inspiration to pen *Family of Warriors*. I trust the words you are about to read will bring honor to those who have sacrificed so much.

In the final stages of this project, I enlisted the help of others to provide suggestions and improvements. I am indebted to Dr. Tom Thompson, Associate Professor of English at the Citadel; John Poggi, a wounded combat veteran; Paul Griffith, LTC, USA (Ret); Sam Boone, Chaplain (Colonel) USA (Ret); Joe Martin, Colonel, USAF (Ret); and Joan Prince for their time and interest in this project. Special thanks must go to Bob Babcock of Deeds Publishing in Athens, Georgia for his unwavering support and encouragement, and to my wife, Susan, for her patience and ability to always keep me grounded in Christian values and principles.

Finally, with all the information available about the events of World War II, I took into account that with any battlefield, two men, standing only steps away from each other, will have different remembrances of the same event, particularly when they recall their impressions years later. Therefore, what you are about to read is my interpretation, and mine alone, of what might have occurred in the traumatic and perilous days of World War II.

INTRODUCTION

AS THE FIRST NOTES OF "TAPS" SPREAD ACROSS THE ROLLING LAND-
scape of Arlington National Cemetery on that spring day, a soft, gentle
breeze comforted those who gathered at the hallowed grounds to celebrate the life of an American who answered the call to serve his country.

The members of the family looked around the flowing landscape
where countless Americans were laid to rest. This family understood
that freedom comes at high cost, for this was a family who ran to the
sound of battle, not away from it. They were a family of warriors.

Throughout the history of our great country, God has blessed us
with many such families; the countless weather-worn crosses and historical makers that dot our land and foreign battlegrounds around the
world give silent yet bold testimony to their willingness to serve for the
common good.

As the ceremony drew to a close and the family left this sacred
site with the flag of our country in their arms, they gazed across the
Potomac at our nation's capital and thought about what this one soldier
had taught them. They knew their memory of him would never die. He
would live in their hearts forever. His example would not fade away.

While the story of this family is not unique in our nation's history, it
is important for us to embrace it, to cherish it, and to retell it over and
over again. The story of this family begins on a crisp Christmas Eve in
1940 when...

CHAPTER ONE

"OH SAY, CAN YOU SEE, BY THE DAWN'S EARLY LIGHT"

World and National Events prior to 24 December 1940

Many factors brought about World War II, from Japan's invasion of Manchuria and China in September 1931 to Hitler's rise to power in Germany in 1933. While the political will in many countries labored to avoid war, aggressive acts by the Japanese in the western Pacific and Southeastern Asia, Germany's occupation of Czechoslovakia, and then their invasion of Poland in 1939, resulted in France and Great Britain declaring war against Germany. Even as the United States announced its neutrality in the European conflict, German forces pushed through the Netherlands, Belgium, and Luxemburg, eventually entering Paris in June 1940. Germany then began an intense aerial bombing campaign against the British Isles. In September 1940, after formally aligning itself with Germany and Japan to create the Axis powers, Italy attacked Greece and then attacked British forces in western Egypt.

Still maintaining its neutrality, the United States provided her allies with military equipment and other supplies as the country took steps to upgrade its military posture to include increasing the number of combat aircraft, building more ships, and passing legislation in September 1940 to begin a peacetime draft for all males age twenty-one to thirty-five.

Christmas Eve, late Tuesday afternoon, 24 December 1940
The Van Ostenburg home, Grand Rapids, Michigan

Jim Van Ostenburg stood on the quiet, tree-lined street looking at his parents' home at 2019 Fulton Street, Grand Rapids, Michigan. The two-story wood and brick residence was similar to many others on this tranquil avenue close to the downtown of this metropolis of over one hundred and seventy thousand, a city known nationally for its blossoming furniture industry. As he studied the home and the well-manicured bushes around it, he thought of all the memories it held for him and his family. Despite the depression and the toll it had taken on his country, his family survived the worst of times and doubt with their dignity intact. His father had been the rock they all relied upon for both direction and strength as each family member pitched in to help earn the money necessary to keep this home safely in their hands. Jim remembered several of the core values his father drilled into all of them during those early depression years: "Pay the price now to enjoy the benefits later. Success only comes from hard work."

Christmas times were especially meaningful to the family even when the depression reached its peak, as his mother insisted that their Christmas tree, even if it was a scrawny limb, stand tall for all to see through their front window. And as the years passed, the trees grew larger and larger, so that on this evening, a fully decorated Scotch pine stood in front of that same large window. And on each window sill on the first floor, candles shone brightly, and an evergreen wreath adorned the center of the front door. A light dusting of new snow from the early evening storm added to this scene, which Norman Rockwell would have been proud to have grace the cover of one of the December editions of *The Saturday Evening Post*.

Though his family expected him at any moment, Jim, his brown uniform jacket now sprouting three chevrons on each sleeve to signify

2

his rank, delayed walking up to the front door. He had so much to tell them. While he was excited and proud of his accomplishments in the last nine months in the United States Army and of the accolades that had come in his direction, there was a degree of anxiety and uncertainty mixed with this exhilaration rumbling about in his soul; he wondered whether he would measure up to the challenges he sensed were ahead. *Will I bring honor to the family name? Will I make them proud?*

But before he could dwell on his concerns any longer, his mother shouted for joy as she threw open the front door. With wet, salty tears streaming down her cheeks, she rushed into her son's arms to enjoy a long, heartfelt embrace, thankful to have him home once again, even if his time with her would be limited, each moment a precious gift to be cherished.

Standing close beside her was his father. Although he was several inches shorter than his son, both men had the same broad shoulders and dark, piercing eyes. Even as the soldier hugged his graceful, lightly gray-headed mother once more, he noted his father's hairline had receded some and the once brown hair was showing signs of starting to thin and gray. After releasing his grasp on his mother, the younger man embraced his father. "Good to see you, Dad."

"You, too, son. You, too. Sergeant's stripes look good on you," the older man said as he inspected his son's uniform. With a glint of pride in his eyes, he smiled. "Come inside. A bit nippy to be standing out here. The rest of the family is waiting. Let me carry your duffel bag."

And with that, the three of them went up the steps into the warm home, to the aroma of pork roast, red potatoes, red cabbage, and a fresh cherry pie baking in the oven, one of Jim's favorite meals. Noise and laughter of the family filled the small dining room, reuniting a mother and father, their five sons, an aunt, and an uncle. The prayers of Ben and Margaret Van Ostenburg had been answered; their oldest son was home. With the concerns of a dark world teetering on the brink of conflict put aside, the family enjoyed the blessings of this Christmas season, their conversations focused on friends and relatives, on days of good times remembered, and upon the blessings provided by Almighty God.

****

With their stomachs full from the savory meal, the men adjourned to the living room while the women busied themselves with cleaning up the dining room and kitchen. Because Margaret's small piano in one corner of the room made seating tight, Ben, Uncle Bud, and Jim sat on the cushioned chairs while the older twins, Jay and Paul, occupied the small couch, leaving the younger set of fraternal twins, Timothy and Michael, to spread themselves out on the wooden floor which was partially covered by a well-worn brown and gold rug. Jim's brothers longed to hear about his exploits since he left for the Army, but it was Uncle Bud, Ben's older brother by two years and a veteran of the Great War, who launched the first flurry of questions as everyone settled down.

"So, Jim, what're they telling you? Any idea where you'll be sent next? You've spent all your time so far in Georgia, right? If the Army is like when your dad and I were in, they'll be shipping you out somewhere soon from all we can gather from the radio, the papers, and what we see on the newsreels at the picture shows. So where'll it be?"

"Well, sir, as you may suspect, there are a lot of rumors flying around. And like in your day, the Army has a way of saying one thing and then changing its mind. One thing for sure, like when you had the draft in the last war, we know the Army will be growing. We may not have much of the new equipment yet, but we're gearing up for more manpower. That's for sure."

"I hear that, but I expect they got something in mind for you. Least

I hope so. The newsreels keep showing the Germans plowing through Europe. Sounds to me like with all that Hitler and the Nazis are doing, taking Poland, sweeping through France, and now bombing the daylights out of London, sooner or later, like it or not, we're gonna get pulled into this thing. Heard somebody say the other day that they've killed almost ten thousand civilians in England in their bombing attacks already. What do you think, Ben? You were a lot closer than me when you faced 'em eyeball-to-eyeball the last time."

He laughed as he finished his thoughts. "Like any good artilleryman, I was back a bit from the front lines, not like you infantry doughboys who were seeing 'em up close. What's your take on all this? We gonna get pulled into this or not?"

All the brothers turned their attention toward their father, a man of few words, and fewer still when it came to telling about his experiences in the Great War. All the boys really knew was that their father had been an infantry soldier in France in 1918 and that he still walked with a slight limp from wounds he received there. Times were few when he would say anything about who, what, where, and when he had served in the war the newspapers described as the "war to end all wars." Would he now give them a glimpse of his experiences?

Ben looked down and touched his wedding ring, moving it around slowly in a circle, a familiar mannerism the boys knew meant he was deep in thought. After a long pause, he answered his brother's question.

"Like it or not, I think Hitler will keep pushing and pushing. When the Germans surrendered in November of '18, their soldiers I saw after that still had a lot of fight in them. They had pride in their country then and from what I see in the newsreels, they've still got that same pride today. From what I gather, the Germans felt the Treaty of Versailles punished them severely. They lost territory, money, prestige, and, not only that, the treaty handcuffed their military. Hurt their ego to the core."

"So you think it's all about losing their pride, their self-esteem?" asked Paul.

"Not all of it certainly, but Hitler's smart. He's playing to their national pride. It seems to me that most Germans feel that he's giving them an opportunity to take care of some unfinished business."

"So you think there's gonna be a war soon?" Jay asked.

"Well, son, for a lot of people in this world, there's a war going full tilt right now. The question is how big will it become, and how many countries will be drawn into it. Sooner or later somebody's got to stand up to 'em. Both the Germans and the Japanese are racking up conquest after conquest. Poland, Holland, Belgium, and France are now in German hands and they're bombing cities in England, like Bud said. And the Japanese have steam-rolled over Korea and China and no one's slowed them down yet."

Ben stopped for a moment before finishing his thoughts. "I'm like you, Bud. I think we'll be dragged into it despite what Roosevelt and those with him who are preaching that we should stay out of it. At least, our president's taking some steps to build up our Armed Forces now and working some deals with England on the Lend Lease program, sending them some ships, trucks, and other equipment. But, seems to me we've got a long ways to go before we're anywhere close to being prepared to get into a big fight."

He paused for a moment before finishing his thoughts. "Like many folks around here, I voted last month for Mr. Willkie to be our next president. Liked the way he was talking tough about standing up to Hitler, but that's not how the election turned out. Since we got Roosevelt again for a third term, we need to pray that he'll get us ready for whatever is ahead."

Michael, the youngest of sons since his twin brother, Timothy, beat him out of the womb by five minutes, spoke out with the enthusiasm of youth. "Well, I know I'm ready to go fight. Me and Tim and all our friends, we've been talking. We're ready to go as soon as we can sign up. We don't want to wait for any draft. Just like Jim. We're ready to go fight 'em now. Yes sir, right now."

Ben and Bud's eyes met for a moment before Ben looked at Michael first before his eyes fell on each of his sons, holding each in his gaze for a time. There was Jim, the most mature; Jay, the sturdiest and perhaps the most capable; Paul, the one with the quickest mind; Timothy, the stoic, the most serious of the five; and Michael, the adventurer, the most impetuous one. Each was strong in both body and character.

"Let me tell each of you something right now. Don't wish for something you know nothing about. Jim, even with all his good training, is just now beginning to understand, but war is something you have to experience to have any true comprehension of what it's all about. Civil War soldiers called it, 'Seeing the elephant.'"

Michael piped up. "What does that mean?"

"Means you have been in close combat. Been under enemy fire. Maybe seen some good friends killed. Means you understand what it's like to know another man is trying to kill you. That's when you've 'seen the elephant.' What it looks and tastes like. What it smells and sounds like. What it feels like deep in your gut when you face it."

"Listen to your father, boys," said Uncle Bud. "He knows what he's talking about. It can turn someone you think is a strong man into a bowl of jelly."

Ben glanced at each of his boys again. "When the bullets start flying, you'll see men you thought were devoid of courage turn into some of the bravest soldiers you can ever imagine. And in seconds you may experience something that will stay with you the rest of your life, something that will keep you awake for more nights than you can count."

The father looked at Michael, his eyes boring into the young man's. "Michael, you and Timothy are close to sixteen. Be glad for the time you now have to score a touchdown or stand at home plate, ready to hit the next fastball out of the park. Be grateful for the time you now have to watch movies and listen to the radio or to dance and sing and to try and figure out what girls are all about. Your time to 'see the elephant' will come soon enough. And when you do, you'll understand what I'm talking about. And you'll be a different person because of the experience."

The silence in the room was deafening, broken only when Ben looked at one of the Army's newest sergeants. "Son, it's time for my evening walk. Care to join me?"

"Of course, Father. It'd be my privilege."

****

"Jim, you haven't asked, but yes, the RCA business is going well. Hard to imagine that I've been working for them for almost three years. Selling phonographs, radios, and records for Radio Corporation of America is different than the clothing industry, but I've enjoyed the change. The company even gave me a plaster "Nipper" dog. Got him standing guard at the front of the store. Get a lot of comments about him, too."

"You mean that mongrel white dog with the black eye?"

"That's him. Really great advertising. Between folks walking in the door to pet him or to touch the 1918 red cherry Victrola near the front window, a number of folks come in, look around, and start to shop. Whoever thought of that make-believe dog is helping us make a reasonable living. Got Paul working there with me, too, since he's got a good mind for what makes those radios work. Might be a good career for him someday."

"Well, Dad, I'm happy for you. You deserve all the best."

The crunch of the snow from the two men's shoes was the only noise either of them made for several blocks before Ben spoke up. "I've never told you much about my soldiering days, have I?"

"No, sir. You never have. I figured you'd get around to it when you felt the time was right. All I really know is that I was born while you were overseas, you were in the infantry, and you got wounded. Like my brothers, I've always been curious."

They strolled along the path for another half block before Ben began to open up. "Your mother and I met while we were growing up in New York City. That's where both our parents settled after they immigrated from the Netherlands around 1892, 1893 or so. Even though we grew up three blocks away from each other, we didn't meet until we were in our late teens."

"Mom has told us a little about that from time to time. She said you were a haberdasher before the war."

"Yeah, that's right, and I was a good one. Did some good tailoring for a number of the New York big shots back in those days. Some of them had a lot of money to throw around and we decked them out real well with some fine material. When the war broke out in Europe and the call came for men to enlist or wait to be drafted, even though your mother and I had been married for a few years, I was one of the two million who enlisted."

"Wow. Guess I didn't realize the number was that high."

"Yeah, there were a lot of men like me and Bud. Felt we owed the country a great deal and joining up was the right the thing to do. Still feel the same today. Got to tell you, it made me very proud when you decided to enlist last year. It's still hard for me to believe that not everyone feels that same way as you and me. Don't know why they can't see serving as a privilege, a sacred duty."

"Yes, sir. I agree. I don't understand it either."

"Your Uncle Bud and I went down to the recruiting office on the same day. He enlisted in the artillery and I enlisted in the infantry. 1st Battalion of the 308th Infantry, 77th Infantry Division. Called the 'Metropolitan Division' since that outfit was made up mostly of men from the New York City area. The unit patch was a Gold Statue of Liberty on a blue background. We took our initial training at Camp Upton over on Long Island. Place was named for General Upton, a Civil War Union general who commanded soldiers at Spotsylvania, Petersburg, and at the third battle of Winchester."

The two men stopped at a corner to let a car pass by. "We sailed to France from the docks there in March 1918. Returned to the same dock thirteen months later but the number of us that came down those steps was a lot fewer than the number that went up them the year before."

Ben was quiet for a few minutes before he went on. "We didn't find out your mother was pregnant with you until January, two months before I was to ship out, and since we didn't know how long I'd be gone, we decided it was best for your mother to move out here to Michigan to be with her sister. Once I got mustered out in May 1919, I headed out here to be with her and we never left. Been blessed to live here since."

Their walk continued for another block. "I worked hard at being a good soldier and so before we left for France, like you, I earned my sergeant's stripes." Ben smiled. "As you know, they don't hand you those stripes for just showing up."

The two men stopped and turned around to head back home as heavier, wet snow began to come down with some bite as bigger flakes swirled around them. "So, Jim, I'm sure you've been training hard: marksmanship, obstacle courses, bayonet drills, all the basic infantry training. How's it going?"

"Good. Spending a lot of time in the field learning how to cope with being cold and wet and miserable."

"Yeah, I remember those days. Don't know who said it, but I've never forgotten that saying, 'If it ain't raining, you ain't training.' Anyway, what do they have in store for you next?"

Jim didn't answer right away, slowing their pace down as they got closer to their warm home as he noticed his father's limp had become more pronounced. "Two things. First, I've asked Betty to marry me and she said yes. We'll get married next week before I head back to Fort Benning—that is, if you'll be my best man."

Ben smiled as he shook his son's hand. "Well, it's about time. She is a wonderful girl, a real charmer. Pretty, too, I might add. You two have known each other for what, four, five years at least? Why that girl is almost part of our family already. And, as far as me being your best man, that would be the greatest honor I've ever had. Of course I will. Does your mother know?"

"No, sir. I wanted to tell you first."

"Well then, we need to get home now before she shoots us both for not telling her."

They were almost to the front door when Jim's father stopped. "You said there were two things. What's the second?"

"No hurry with that one, Dad. We'll talk more tomorrow. I see Mom is looking out the window, so I'd better go spend some time with her before I get us both in really big trouble."

Christmas Day, Wednesday afternoon, 25 December 1940
The Van Ostenburg home, Grand Rapids, Michigan

It had been a clear, crisp day. The snow had stopped during the night, leaving a pristine blanket of unblemished white covering the lawn. It was a day full of festivities, not only because of the celebration of Jesus Christ's birth and of the giving of gifts, but also due to the presence of Jim back in the home, all wrapped around the grand news that he and Betty would be married within a week. Despite all the meal preparations and the myriad of details running through her head, Margaret could not stop smiling. She fluttered about like a bird on a spring day going from tree to tree looking for food, hugging Jim first and then

Betty and then Jim again. "A week," she gasped. "You've only given Betty's family a week to plan for the reception, the guests, the church..."

"Mother, don't worry. Everything is under control. Before I came home yesterday, Betty and I went by the church and reserved the time. We want a simple family wedding. There are a few small details to work out, but we've taken care of the basics. You know: who, what, where, when."

"Yes, but..."

"Everything will be fine. Right after the wedding, we'll only have a few days together before I head back to Georgia, but we've got everything under control." He quieted her concerns with another long hug. "I love you, Mom. I'll be back in a little while. Right now my best man and I have a few things to talk about. Get your list of questions ready for Betty and me and we'll tackle them when I get back from my walk with Dad. Trust me. It will be a wonderful wedding. Simple, yet full of honor for our vows. Be back soon."

****

"As one infantryman to another, can you tell me some of what you went through in France?"

Ben knew the questions would come sooner or later, but before he could utter a sound, a pigeon suddenly appeared in the sky, attracting his attention. He watched it for a long time until the bird disappeared behind some tall pines.

"We'd been surrounded for six days. Almost no food left. We'd stripped everything we could from the dead: food, ammunition, bandages, water. The Germans kept probing our perimeter every day and every night, trying to find a weak spot and to make sure we'd never get any rest. Sometimes the attacks were small; sometimes much larger. Sometimes at first light; other times at dusk. They came close to breaking through a couple of times. It was always a close-in fight, a few times hand-to-hand, but mostly at twenty-five to fifty yards or so. Like us, the Krauts were battle-tested and they used every fold in the ground to try and gain an advantage. They kept hollering for us to give up, to surrender."

Jim stayed quiet for a moment as he tried to picture the battlefield Ben was describing. "Must have been tough."

"Yes, it was, son... yes, it was. On the sixth day, artillery began to fall right on us. After a few minutes of this barrage, Major Whittlesey, our commanding officer, figured we were being shelled by our own guns miles away. Seemed that they had no idea where we were or even if our unit still existed, which meant that none of our messengers or other carrier pigeons had gotten through. Anyway, the major wrote a quick message and released a carrier pigeon. I remember hearing someone say that was the last one we had. We all watched that bird as it flew away, praying it would get through. Not long after that, the artillery stopped. Shortly before dark, one of our sister units broke through the German lines and we were saved."

Ben walked slower as he reflected more on those days again. "Never should have happened, but like a lot of things in war, you must always expect the unexpected. Our battalion was part of the Meuse-Argonne Offensive. The 92nd Infantry Division was to attack on our right and a French unit was to advance on our left. As we found out later, neither of those units moved as fast as us and that's how we got cut off. Sitting out there by ourselves, no friendly units anywhere near us. Totally on our own."

The old soldier stared straight ahead. "Soon as the Germans figured it out, they closed in on us and hit us with everything they had. MG 08 machine guns. A lot of grenades, 'potato mashers' we called them. Thankfully, they didn't use any gas. Guess they figured they'd be gassing themselves along with us if they did. Anyway, in no time we were a collection of dead and wounded, barely hanging on. Hard to forget all those moans and cries for help, hoping somebody would find us. Took me a long time to put most of that behind me, but I've learned you never really get over an experience like that."

"How many men made it out of there?"

Ben stared straight ahead before he finally answered the question. "Saw a newspaper article some time back about us. They called us 'The Lost Battalion.' The article said that there were 550 of us when the battle began. Only 190 of us came out alive. The rest were dead, POWs, or missing. Three or four men, I can't recall which, were awarded the Medal of Honor for what they did there. From what I saw, that number could have easily been doubled or tripled. I served with many brave, honorable men. Half of the men in my squad died there. The rest of us were wounded."

As they continued to trudge slowly through the snow, Jim asked, "Ever see any of those men after you got back home?"

"No. Once we landed back in New York, along with a few of my fellow NCOs, we went by to see the parents and loved ones of some of the men killed to tell them what happened. After a week or two of doing that, as soon as I was mustered out, I joined your mother here. I get a letter every now and then from a few of those I knew quite well, but I haven't seen any of them in over twenty years."

The two men stopped for a moment near a park with several small hills. They watched silently as several boys, probably seven or eight years old, gleefully raced down the hills on the new sleds they got for Christmas earlier in the day. Neither man spoke for a long time as they watched the boys test the fresh snow over and over.

"After the war, Major Whittlesey received a number of well-earned accolades including the Medal of Honor, but I think the loss of so many men under his command must have weighed heavy on his heart. A few years later, 1921 I think it was, he jumped overboard from an ocean liner as it was crossing the Atlantic. I read he left a note, but I could be wrong about that. From my perspective, he saved 190 men."

Ben paused for a long time before he finished his thoughts. "I wish even to this day that I had somehow, somewhere been able to tell him that. Still pulls at my guts to know I didn't do that. Maybe if I had taken time to talk with him or written him a letter, I could have saved his life like he saved mine."

After a few more minutes of neither man saying a word, they turned around to head back to the house. It was Jim who broke their silence. "You asked me what is next for me. With all the preparations going on in the Army for a possible war, they're going to start an Officer Candidate School at Fort Benning this summer. The captain in my unit wants me to apply, so I've decided to put my paperwork in when I get back. They're calling it OCS. Will be around ninety days long. After graduation we'll be brand new lieutenants and we'll be sent out to units who are short officers. Least that's the scuttlebutt right now."

"Is that the second big thing you were going to tell me yesterday?"

"Yes, sir. Betty already knows and so she's prepared for whatever may come. She'll probably come to Benning at some point if we're allowed to do that, so we can spend what time we can together as this whole thing evolves. A lot of variables right now, but that's our plan."

"Well, that's all you can do for now. As far as you becoming an officer, I am not sure what advice an old sergeant can give you except maybe for a few things I learned in those woods in France."

"At this point I'll take whatever you can give me."

"Well, there's one thing I remember that supposedly came from an old German general. Said that no matter how good your preparation is before the battle, most plans never survive the first shot in combat. He was saying that what appears to be a good, solid plan comes apart real quick when the bullets start flying around, so stay flexible. Be ready to adapt as the situation changes."

"I've heard some of that already but it doesn't hurt to hear it again."

Ben looked at his son. "Now that you've got my brain working, here's another thing. As those of us in my battalion learned, never lose hope. As long as you can take a breath, keep fighting. You never know when help might be right around the next bend in the road."

Jim's head bobbed up and down. "Got it. Other thoughts?"

"Yeah, here's another one. In combat, you'll normally be faced with several options. The tendency is to over-think the problem, taking too long trying to find the perfect solution. And so when leaders take too long to make a decision, it always means dead soldiers. This is particularly true the closer you are to the enemy. Remember, a bad plan executed vigorously is always better than no plan at all. So when you're in a bad spot, do something."

Ben stood still, staring deeply into his son's face. "Now, one more thought, then I'll stop. It comes from the Bible, not an Army field manual. In the first chapter of Joshua, God tells Joshua over and over, 'Be strong and courageous.' He then reminds Joshua that He will be with him wherever he goes. Think about that. God promises He will be with us wherever we go, but we've got to trust Him. You got that?"

"Yes, sir."

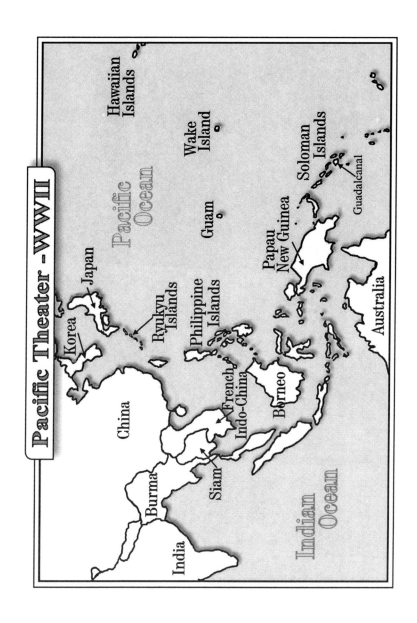

CHAPTER TWO

"WHAT SO PROUDLY WE HAILED"

World and National Events between Christmas Day 1940 and 26 September 1941

During the spring of 1941, major land battles take place in North Africa between British and Italian forces reinforced by German forces. The German Army also advances into Yugoslavia and the island of Crete before invading the Soviet Union in early summer, 1941. Meanwhile, Japan continues to consolidate its gains in conquered lands while preparing for their next advances. British and Axis forces clash in major sea battles in the Atlantic.

The United States continues its public stand of neutrality while continuing to send arms and material to its allies. With Congressional approval, President Roosevelt increases the budget for military spending, tightens the exportation of oil and aviation fuel, freezes Japanese assets, and extends the draft period from one year to thirty months.

1000 hours, Thursday morning, 27 September 1941
Post Parade Field, Fort Benning, Georgia

The day dawned bright and warm, quite different from what Ben and Margaret experienced the day before as they traveled south, when pelting rains and blustery winds seemed, at times, almost powerful enough to blow their rail car off the track. Their journey to Georgia started before dawn on Wednesday in Grand Rapids on the Pennsylvania Railroad. After their first major stop in Cincinnati, they boarded a Louisville & Nashville train that took them through Knoxville and Atlanta before reaching their destination of Columbus, Georgia late in the evening. Despite the small accommodations Jim had arranged for them in this sleepy town of forty thousand, they awoke refreshed, ready to meet Betty at the ceremony site on Fort Benning, ten miles south of their lodging. Upon their arrival at the post by cab, they greeted their daughter-in-law with open arms. This was a day of great celebration for their oldest son.

****

The command, "Commppaannyy... Preesseenntt... Arms!" rolled across the large, freshly mowed parade field located across Wold Avenue from Infantry Hall, an imposing white two-story building. The graduates of the first United States Army's Officer Candidate School stood rock steady before bleachers filled to capacity on both sides of the large reviewing stand.

Margaret whispered in Ben's ear, "Why do they give the commands like that? All their words stretched out so?"

Ben studied the formation with a practiced eye before answering. Each man looked like a recruiting poster: right hand and arm held at the correct angle of a salute, feet facing outward at a forty-five degree angle, head still, eyes fixed on a point directly ahead, backbones ramrod straight. No movement or wavering disturbed their ranks. "For every command, there is a preparatory command to get the men ready for what is called the command of execution. It's done that way so that each member of the unit performs the command precisely at the same time."

Before Margaret could comment further, the voice over the loud speaker announced, "Ladies and Gentlemen, please rise and render the appropriate honors at the playing of our National Anthem."

Ben and Margaret immediately rose to their feet along with Betty and all those in the large crowd. While the two women shifted their eyes slightly to the right and left to take in the entire scene, Ben stood at attention, his hands down the seams of his newly purchased black suit, his highly polished shoes reflecting the sun's light, his hands cupped, his eyes fixed on the flag of his country, a soft breeze blowing the red, white, and blue silk softly to and fro. At the sound of the band's first notes of "The Star Spangled Banner," his right arm snapped upward, his posture and actions mirroring those around him who wore the uniform of the United States of America.

When the song ended, the unit commander gave the command, "Orrddeerr... Arms!" and then, "Paarraaddee... Rest," each order executed by all members of the OCS class with absolute precision. With all members of the unit standing motionless with their hands behind their backs in a knife-like position, a distinguished-looking colonel in his brown jacket and khaki pants uniform known as pinks and greens walked to the podium at the front of the reviewing stand, thanking the many visitors who had come to witness this day's historic event. This officer then made a special note that the large football stadium to their left was named Doughboy Stadium, in honor of the fallen soldiers of the Great War. Then he asked all those former Doughboys in the audience to stand and be recognized.

The number that stood with Ben was great and the applause for these veterans lasted for several minutes.

After the crowd quieted down, the officer stated that this was a great moment for the United States Army as this was the first Officer Candidate School class to complete the newly designed course specifically to fill the ranks of Second Lieutenants required for the Army's expansion. This officer than gave a short introduction of the speaker who would give the graduation address.

Even though Ben had never heard of the man who was to deliver the message, he noticed that, while the man's physical appearance was unremarkable, his military bearing and his strong eyes seemed to capture every person in attendance. Not far into his address, Ben judged Brigadier General Omar N. Bradley, Commandant of the United States Army Infantry School, to be a leader he could have followed in France as the man's mannerisms and words gave every indication he was a man of integrity and valor, a man of courage and strong beliefs. To Ben's way of thinking, Bradley appeared to be a soldier's soldier.

***

The Officers' Club, located a short walking distance from the parade field, played host to the reception. As soon as the graduates and their families arrived, the decorations and food samplings seized the attention of all the ladies, including Margaret and Betty, as the varieties and presentations of shrimp, carved beef, vegetables, salads and desserts filled the throng of serving tables to capacity. The Army's celebration for its newest officers far exceeded the norms of the day as many recalled the hardship and despair of the last century's economic distress.

As the two women chatted away with other proud mothers, wives, and other close friends of the graduates, Ben and Jim found themselves seated at a well-decorated table of Infantry blue in the large ballroom. Joining them was another newly-commissioned lieutenant and his father, a businessman from Paterson, New Jersey, an owner of a car dealership that specialized in Fords and Packards. Richard Adams was his name. Thomas was his son.

As soon as introductions were made, the short, rotund businessman began a conversation with Ben. "I'm sure you're mighty proud of your son, just like I am of mine. It seems to me that after these boys put the Germans and Japanese in their place, they'll be treated to a heroes' welcome. With all the businesses we have in our country, they'll be clamoring for their expertise and leadership. Yes sir, this war that's coming will open up opportunities for these boys, no doubt about it. That the way you see it, Ben?"

Ben took a slow sip of water from his glass before responding. "Well, Richard, that's not something I've considered. From my perspective, I just want these men to serve their country honorably and come home safe and sound. My fear is that, based on the powder keg the world seems to be sitting on these days, if it explodes, a world war will be long and bloody. Far more costly than we experienced twenty years ago."

The businessman's eyes widened. "Oh, come on. You can't be serious. You heard what that general said. 'We're delivering aircraft and equipment to England... The Army is growing in size... We're shipping material to China... Training some men right here at Fort Benning to be paratroopers to take the fight to the enemy.' With those initiatives ongoing and with men like these in this room in our Armed Forces, the countries who are stirring up trouble will run for cover as soon as they see American colors confronting them."

Ben stared down at his hands, remembering, fingering his ring. "You really think so?" he asked as he noted that both sons remained quiet as they observed the discussion.

"Yes. Of course, I do. We're just too strong for them, too industrialized, too much of a world power. Those countries will stop all this nonsense about world domination as soon as we enter the fight, believe you me."

Ben looked out the window, the red, white, and blue flag swaying gently in the breeze in front of the Officers' Club before he turned to study the man. They were close in age. As Ben inspected the cut of the man's clothes, he recognized the expensive quality of the material. Suspecting he already knew the answer, he asked, "Let me ask you, Richard, what unit did you serve with in during the Great War?"

The businessman sputtered, "Well, I... I served on the home-front. My contribution was making vehicles for the war effort."

Ben paused, asking himself, *How did this man manage to avoid the draft? Influence of a relative or some loophole? No matter. Why is it that some let others fight for our country while they sit on the sidelines and suck on the public mammary? Since everyone in our society receives the benefit of victory, how can any man in good conscience let others go in his place?*

"Well, I'm sure your efforts were most helpful. Because of our victory twenty years ago, it seems to me that Germany, Japan, and Italy would like to have their names be considered in any discussion about the great nations of the world."

"Yes, but..."

Ben continued without pause. "When we consider that right now, their military forces are much larger than ours, and with their recent successes, they must be brimming with confidence. Coupled with their proven military equipment, that is a dangerous combination. In many ways, it is almost like they're looking to take us on. To flex their muscles. To test their strength against ours."

Adams scoffed at Ben's remarks as he tried to recover and save face in front of the two young men sitting next to them. "I can't buy into that. I still believe that when we enter the fight full bore, Germany and Japan will back away. We're too much of a world power for them to stand up to us."

"Richard, twenty years ago, when we first arrived in France, I saw too many men die because we thought we knew everything about war.

In truth, we were neophytes. Too cocky. Too sure of ourselves. And because of my experiences of machine gun bullets zipping past, artillery rounds ripping great holes in the dirt, the smell of phosgene gas, and the cries of wounded and dying men, I shudder to think what our sons may face in the days ahead. While, like you, I pray for a quick resolution, my familiarity with what may come their way causes me grave concern."

Adams shook his head. "While I respect your opinion, sir, it's still hard for me to believe that these other countries will not..." stopping in mid-sentence when he realized that General Bradley was visiting each table, congratulating the new lieutenants, and their table was next in line.

As the general approached, the four men leaped to their feet. Without a moment's hesitation, Adams reached into his pocket for his business card which, upon Bradley's arrival at their table, he thrust into the officer's hand.

"General, my name is Richard Adams, from Paterson, New Jersey. It is my great pleasure to meet you, sir."

Bradley looked first at the young officers and said, "As you were, gentlemen," before he glanced at the card. "Thank you, Mr. Adams. I trust you gentlemen will pardon my interruption, but I wanted to come over and congratulate these two new officers. They have shown themselves to be the kind of men we need in the days ahead and you two can be very proud of their accomplishments."

The businessman beamed. "Thank you, General. I'm sure under your leadership, these men have learned a great deal."

The general studied Adams for a moment before he turned in Ben's direction. Holding out his hand, Bradley said, "Mr. Van Ostenburg, I owe you an apology. After I finished my remarks today, I realized I had made a great oversight."

"General, I'm sorry... I don't understand."

"Well, sir, I consider it a privilege that when a man who served our country as you did in France comes on this post, I believe it is my duty to acknowledge your contribution to our country. It is not often I have the honor to shake the hand of a man who was a member of the 1st Battalion of the 308th Infantry. Thank you for the example you and your unit have given to those of us who are in uniform."

Ben stared at the man for a long time before he nodded. "General, I appreciate your thoughts, but the honor belongs to our brothers who did not come home. They will remain in France forever."

Bradley gazed into the old soldier's eyes. "You are right. We lost many good men during those times." The general stood still for a moment before looking at James and then back at his father. "You've raised a good man, Ben. He'll make you proud."

Ben could only nod his head in agreement as Bradley patted him on the back before he moved on to the next table. When the general was out of hearing, James said, "Dad, I didn't know you knew General Bradley."

"Never met the man before today, son. Men in his position know a great deal more about the history of our Army than most. Looks like a good man to serve with, doesn't he?"

Richard Adams, who had been closely following the dialogue between Bradley and Van Ostenburg, nodded his head in Ben's direction before he left the table without any additional comments, his son following in his wake.

After he watched the two men leave, Jim spoke up. "Got my orders last week."

"That's good, son. Some place you and Betty can start enjoying some time together or will it be in some far-off exotic land?"

"Well, let's just say, it's not what we hoped for. Most of my classmates are going to be stationed at training posts in the States, but for me and a few others, we're heading overseas right away. Betty's been quite good today about holding back her tears. Our plans are that, after

I out-process from here tomorrow or the next day, we'll be taking a train to Los Angeles. We'll spend a week or so together there before I ship out. She'll then head back to Grand Rapids and move back in with her folks. Maybe even look to get her old job back. It's been really hard on her here with us seeing each other only on weekends for a few hours, but we've managed to make the most out of it. There are a few other couples like us so the girls have been getting by all right, but now..."

"You never said where you'd be going."

"The Philippines."

"And your assignment?"

"I'll be in one of the infantry battalions of the 43rd Infantry Regiment, Philippine Scouts. A mixed battalion as I understand it. Some U.S. and some Filipinos."

The two men sat still for a few minutes, the father absorbing his son's words. "In that case, since we don't have much time, you mind if this old sergeant gives some more advice to one of the Army's newest 'butter' bars?"

"Don't mind a bit. Fact is, I was hoping you would."

"All right then... What does the term 'situational awareness' mean to you?"

"I'd say it means to use all your senses all the time. Keep your eyes and ears open, always looking around and listening. Be constantly aware of your surroundings."

"Pretty good, but I'd add a few things. First, know that situational awareness is a learned art. The more you practice it, the better you'll get at it. And as you do, you'll become more aware of the subtle changes that are occurring around you. Second, if something doesn't sound right or look right, chances are, it isn't. Assume nothing. The bottom line of this is keep moving your head on a swivel, always looking, moving your eyes around you every second. The object of this is to avoid getting surprised. Remember the enemy is looking for you just like you are looking

27

for him. The enemy will be a thinking man, just like you, so don't ever take him for granted."

"Thanks. I got it."

"Oh, and more thing since you are now an officer. Remember that in many cases, the only things that get done are what the boss checks or causes to be checked."

Before Ben could offer any more thoughts, he spotted Margaret and Betty heading their way. Based on the looks on the two women's faces, he didn't have to guess too much about their latest conversation. He knew it would be a tearful ride back to Grand Rapids.

Friday afternoon, 28 September 1941
Aboard a train traveling north through Tennessee

"Ben, you stay up with the world situation far more than me, so tell me what this means about Jim going to the Philippines. What's so important there that it requires sending my son? Doesn't the Army have any compassion for families and newly-married young folks? I just don't understand."

Margaret continued to stare out the window of the train as they passed through the same hills and small towns of southeastern Tennessee they sped through two days earlier. "What's so important about those islands anyway? After talking with the other mothers, most of Jim's classmates will be stationed at other posts around the country—Texas, California, Colorado, or staying in Georgia. Why are they sending Jim to some dreadful place in the Pacific Ocean out in the middle of nowhere? And without Betty? Why are they doing that to him?"

Ben watched a man plow his field of corn on his small plot of land as the train began its slow approach into Knoxville before he attempted to answer the barrage of questions his wife had fired in his direction.

"I can't tell you any of the specifics of why Jim is going there, but he did share with me that those who finished highest in his class are all headed there. That tells me our son was one of the best in his class and the Army wants to use his talents right away."

"But the Philippines? Why does our country even care about what happens there? What's so important about that place?"

"I don't have all the answers to your questions except to say that over forty years ago or so, those islands came under the protection of the United States and we've had military forces there ever since. And with all the Japanese advances throughout Southeast Asia, our government wants to make sure the Japanese government understands the United States of America has a vested interest in those islands. Why, we've even got the former Chief of Staff of the Army, General McArthur, there advising the Philippine government and their military. And, as you can imagine, with Jim going there, I'll certainly be paying much more attention to that part of the world."

Margaret looked at her husband for a long time before responding, "All right, I can accept that. Our country feels those islands are important, but why is my Jim going there?"

"Now, Margaret, you know the answer to that. Like it or not, he's not just your Jim anymore. He's an officer in the United States Army. He goes where and when he is ordered. It's just that simple. He is serving for the good of the country and while we may have concerns about where he serves and for his welfare, I'm proud of his willingness to do his duty."

Margaret remained silent for a long time as she stared out the window without any focus on the city they were passing through. "You're right, of course. But after what you went through in France, hasn't our family paid its dues?"

She then looked straight into her husband's eyes. "I've heard you and Bud talk. You're both saying that with all that the Germans and the

ED DEVOS

Japanese and the Italians are doing, we'll be involved in a war sooner or later. And it scares me. First, Jim is going to the Pacific on some islands I can't even spell. Then it will be Jay and Paul. And then my babies, Timothy and Michael. I know what I felt like as a young wife when you were in France. And I know what I'm feeling as a mother. Am I wrong to want to hold my children tight? To protect them and wish to keep them out of any danger?"

The old soldier wrapped his arms around his wife as the tears began to flow down her checks. He held her for a long time. *Now is not the time to tell her I've been told that with all the rumors of war whirling about, our country will be forming Rationing Boards. And the city officials have nominated me to be on the Grand Rapids board. Since others are doing their part, it's the least I can do. Serving our country is not something done once.*

The Good Book said it best. "Everyone to whom much is given, of him much will be required." Our family has been blessed. We have been given much. Therefore, it is now our time to give once again to the land that has given us so much. It is our duty. Protect my son, Oh, Lord. Please protect him.

Margaret, too, was deep in thought. *First, my husband was a warrior for our country, and now my son will be as well. And like it or not, if war comes, my other sons will follow. They're so much like their father. They will not hesitate to do their duty. Lord, help me brace for whatever is before us.*

30

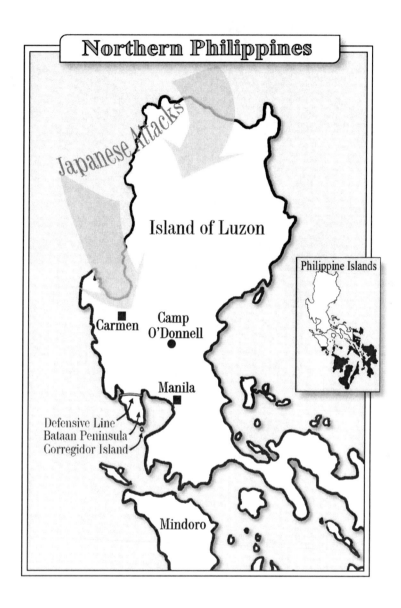

Northern Philippines

Japanese Attacks

Island of Luzon

Philippine Islands

Carmen

Camp
O'Donnell

Manila

Defensive Line
Bataan Peninsula
Corregidor Island

Mindoro

CHAPTER THREE

"AT THE TWILIGHT'S LAST GLEAMING"

World and National Events between 29 September 1941 and Christmas Day 1941

During the fall of 1941, the German Army continues its march eastward into the Soviet Union and begins a siege of Leningrad which lasts for nine hundred days. During their advance, German forces massacre over 33,000 Jews in Kiev, Ukraine. On 7 December, Japan launches a surprise attack on Pearl Harbor, Hawaii, destroying four battleships and eleven other ships, along with 247 airplanes, and killing over 2,330 Americans. Within a few days of the Pearl Harbor attack, the Japanese attack Wake Island, the Philippines, Guam, Midway, the Malay Peninsula, and Hong Kong, the colonial gem of the British Empire.

The United States declares war on Japan, and its allies under the Tripartite Pact, Germany and Italy. President Roosevelt calls 7 December "a date which will live in infamy."

Thursday morning, 25 December 1941
Near Carmen on the island of Luzon, Philippines

As the first signs of dawn appeared in the eastern skies, six Nambu machine guns, each weapon capable of firing up to five hundred rounds a minute, opened up on the American position. Supported by this barrage of hot lead, the Japanese infantry, many of whom were battle-hardened veterans of the campaigns in China, rushed the perimeter once more through the vine-covered, dense jungle.

Assaulting first one flank and then the other, they steadily gained ground against the 43rd Philippine Scout Infantry Regiment, a mix of American and Filipino soldiers. Jim Van Ostenburg had lost count of how many times he and his men had faced these onslaughts the past few days, but he knew his company's numbers were dwindling from each attack. Worse, he sensed no signs of any let-up in the Japanese advance.

It had been two weeks since General Masaharu Homma's 14th Japanese Army made an amphibious assault onto the beaches of the north and northwestern sides of Luzon, the largest of the Philippine islands. Even though it seemed from Jim's perspective that General MacArthur had sufficient warning of the impending attack, American and Filipino preparations proved to be inadequate at best, deplorable at worst, as the Japanese bombers caught MacArthur's B-17 bombers stationed at Clark Air Base napping on the first day of the battle, destroying almost all of the "Flying Fortresses" as they sat on the ground only a few hours after the Japanese attacked Pearl Harbor.

Coupled with reports he had heard earlier that the Japanese had also forced their way onto Guam and Wake Island, Jim felt the only thing he could do was to fight a delaying action with the men still with him against this determined enemy, standing his ground for as long as practical, retreating when necessary, all to protect his force as best he could. To do otherwise would be unforgiveable.

****

When another bullet snapped past him, an inch or two over his head, Sergeant Ramsey called out, "Japs flanking us on the left. Trying to get behind us!"

Jim took a quick look in that direction, spotting some soldiers dressed in dark green uniforms bobbing and weaving quickly through the dense jungle underbrush. "I see 'em. On three, blast 'em with everything we got. Then pull everyone back to that stream to our rear."

"You mean the one about five minutes behind us?"

"That's the one. I'll cover you first. We'll try and make another stand there... Got to keep working our way south. Next big defensive line is supposed to be ten, fifteen miles back that way. Near Paniqui."

"You sure we can last that long?"

"No, but we gotta try. You ready?"

"Yes, sir. I guess," Ramsey nodded before he hollered out to the men who could hear him amidst the gunfire that now split the air from several directions. "On three, fire everything you got and run south for the stream behind us."

For a second, Van Ostenburg recalled the words of one of his instructors during his OCS training. *Candidates, make sure you take time to assess the situation before you act. Consider all your courses of action before making a decision. Then issue your orders in a calm, confident manner so that your subordinate leaders clearly understand what you want them to do. This will ensure they have confidence in your abilities.*

What BS! Well-intentioned school-house doctrine like that sounded good on a small hilltop on the northeastern reaches of Fort Benning in August with no one shooting at you, but now? Now it was a question of doing something, anything, and doing it now, like dad said. Don't waste time. Do something. Methodically considering various options will mean certain death. Got to do something now!

"One... two... three!!! Fire!!!

Without a second to spare, the men around the lieutenant cut loose with all the rounds they had in their magazines before sprinting to the rear. It was the second time in the last two days they used this same maneuver. From Jim's perspective, it was the only tactic keeping them alive.

****

Three more times, Jim and his men fell back in a similar manner from the hordes facing them. Unbeknownst to Van Ostenburg, he and his men and the units to his right and left faced General Homma's main attack, whose mission was to destroy all American and Filipino forces in central Luzon.

During a pause in the action, Jim thought, *Three days ago I was the junior officer in a company of six officers and one hundred and fifty soldiers. Now, I'm the only officer left. The company a fraction of what it was. No telling where the men we left behind are. Wounded, captured, tortured, dead; perhaps in that sequence, perhaps not. Can't worry about them now. Got to keep moving. Got to keep those with me alive. Can't lose hope. Can't quit. Got to keep moving. To stop is to die.*

As nightfall began to settle in, Van Ostenburg sent out scouts to his right and left in hopes of making contact with some other friendly elements, but the jungle was too thick, too unforgiving to gouge around in it for any length of time, so his scouts returned with nothing positive to report. Even though he had heard gunfire at some distance on both his left and right flanks off and on throughout the day, he could draw no conclusions from those sounds.

Without any radio contact or messengers from any higher authority, Jim grabbed Ramsey and the other sergeant still with him. "OK, here's the plan. Redistribute what ammo we've got so everybody has about the same amount. Soon as it gets a little darker, we're heading south and hope we bump into some of our own guys. Can't stay here. The Japs will be trying to sneak up on us in the dark. Tell your guys that when we move, be as quiet as you can. I'll lead. You two keep everybody moving at my pace as best as you can. Any questions?"

"Yeah. What if we take fire, say from the right?"

"Then we'll move left for fifty yards and then head south again. In other words, break contact by moving in the opposite direction of the fire and then head south again. The running password will be "Tigers" for the Detroit Tigers. Even our Filipinos should be able to handle that. If we get separated, gather what men you can and keep moving south. We'll try and sort it all out once we get some daylight. Any other ideas?"

Ramsey nodded, "Works for me, LT."

"Good. Now brief your guys and get ready to move. Get in tight while we can still see each other so nobody gets lost at the start. We'll start moving in ten minutes." The lieutenant looked at Sergeant Ramsey. "I want you to be the last man in the formation. Keep everybody in front of you."

"Got it. Oh, LT. One more thing."

"Yeah? What's that?"

"Merry Christmas."

Thursday afternoon, 25 December 1941
The Van Ostenburg home, Grand Rapids, Michigan

As everyone moved to the dining room table, Ben looked around at the others: Margaret, Jay, Paul, Timothy, and Michael. At the far end of the table stood Ben's brother, Bud, and Betty, Jim's wife. Everyone's head was down, each feeling a bit awkward, not knowing what to say or how to say it, each caught up in the emotions of the last few weeks.

While he understood their discomfort, for Ben, it was time to move forward. "Before we eat this meal, I want us to remain standing for a moment... Now hold each other's hand."

After making sure everyone followed his instructions, the patriarch of the family stood up straight. "Before we eat, let's pause for a moment and reflect. We all know what happened these past few weeks: Pearl Harbor; the concerns we have for Jim and the soldiers with him; the sadness we feel for Bud and the loss of his dear Joanne; and the uncertainty of the world situation and the responsibility that must weigh heavy upon President Roosevelt."

He glanced around to make sure he had all of them in his grasp before he continued. "Above everything else, let's remember that God holds the whole world in His hands. As best we can, let's focus on the hope that a little baby born in a humble manger brought us long ago. Many years ago I learned that no matter how dire the circumstances may seem, God is always with us. He is in charge. Remember that. Now, Jay, as the oldest son with us here today, please pray for our meal."

****

While Ben's encouragement brought a ray of light to his household, other American households wrestled with their emotions throughout the day. Their discussions and thoughts were a mixture of rage and fury, terror and fright, panic and alarm, distrust and doubt, glumness and pessimism.

As the women were about to clear all the dishes from the table and the men reassembled in the living room, Ben cleared his throat.

"A few days ago I got a copy of the President's speech to Congress from 8 December. I think it would be appropriate for you to hear his words. To my way of thinking, he is both truthful and optimistic. He understands that as a nation, we'll fight for causes we believe in. And as a nation, while we do not seek war, when it visits our doorstep, we will accept the challenge like the warriors of old."

Ben then unfolded the paper and stared at it for a moment. "As you know, I didn't vote for the president, but from what I have heard from him in the last few weeks, I think he has got a good handle on where we go from here as a nation. Listen to just a few of his words."

'No matter how long it may take us to overcome this premeditated invasion, the American people in their righteous might will win through to absolute victory...I believe I interpret the will of the Congress and of the people when I assert that we will not only defend ourselves to the uttermost, but will make very certain that this form of treachery shall never endanger us again... Hostilities exist... There is no blinking at the fact that our people, our territory, and our interests are in grave danger... With confidence in our armed forces—with the unbounded determination of our people—we will gain the inevitable triumph—so help us God.'

Ben laid the paper down. "I'll leave this copy here if you care to read the president's words for yourselves."

****

"Dad?"

"Yes, Jay. What is it?"

Jay, now a man of almost twenty with broad shoulders and trim figure, worked for the Canteen Company, a growing enterprise now spreading its wings in the Grand Rapids area as it provided pre-packaged food items to the various locations around the city's industrial sector. He looked at his twin brother, Paul, who stood next to him, before answering his father's questioning glance.

"The two of us have been talking. We know guys like us are gonna get drafted sooner or later. We're the right age. Not married. And we're in good health. We figure if we wait to be drafted, we might end up some place we don't like, doing something we don't want to do. So we're thinking, if we enlist soon, we have a better chance of having some say in what we'd be doing in the service. What do you think?"

Ben looked at his brother Bud before he responded. "Well, there is some logic in what you're saying. Tell me, what exactly are you two thinking you'd like to do in the service? You're both smart and have some leadership and technical skills, so there are many things you could do. Obviously, you've got some ideas so what are you two thinking?"

Paul was first to respond, his words coming rapidly, like a machine gun burst, just like he practiced. "I wanna fly. Dad, we've talked about this a while back after you took us to that air show a few years ago over in Lansing. After we got home that night, it was all I could think about — getting up in the air like those men we watched that day. That's my dream."

"I remember, son. Sounds like you've got your mind pretty well made up."

"Yes, sir. And since I've been working for you this past year, you know I've got a good mind for mechanical things. I figure as good as I am with radios and things like that, it should help get me in the door for the Army Air Corps. I know I'd be leaving you in a bind at the store, but like Jay said, if we don't volunteer soon, we're gonna get drafted anyway. And if that happens, I might lose my chance to fly. You volunteered when you were around our age and we want to do the same."

Ben sat back in his chair, a non-committal look on his face. "You want to fly, too, Jay?"

"No, sir. From what I've seen in the war clips at the movie theater, I think I'd like to be in the tank corps. Something that travels fast, has big guns, and gives you a chance to take the fight to the enemy. I know you were in the infantry and Jim is doing that, but for me, I think I'd like to give tanks a try."

Jay laughed, "I've got more brains than Paul. I wanna stay on the ground instead of thinking I'm some kind of bird flittering around in the sky somewhere."

Ben smiled as he looked over at his brother. "Your thoughts, Bud?"

The old artilleryman looked at his nephews. "Like we've said for a while, we felt this day would come sooner or later. Even though Roosevelt's tried his best to keep us out of it, when the Japs attacked Pearl Harbor, they gave us no choice but to declare war on 'em and the Germans and the Italians as well. And so now, everyone needs to step up. Time for men to be men."

Bud stopped for a moment before a bit of a grin spread across his face. "Ben, like you, I'm mighty proud of these two. The only thing I'll say is that I'm glad I'll not be the one to tell Margaret. Maybe, since these two want to do the right thing and be courageous and bold, they should be the ones to tell their mother. Yes, sir. That's what I think."

****

Later that night when he went out to the kitchen, Ben found Jim's wife crying. When he wrapped his arms around her, she crumpled in his arms. "Mr. Van, what can I do? Where can I turn? We haven't heard a word about Jim. Don't know if he's dead or alive. Why won't they tell us something?" She looked up at her father-in-law. "Why won't the Army tell me something?"

Ben looked into the young woman's eyes as he wiped the tears from her cheeks. He longed for her to call him "Dad," but since she had known him for so long as "Mr. Van," he could accept that, particularly now.

"Oh, child, it's only been a few weeks since all this started. The Army will tell us when they know something. Right now, they have lots of families asking the same questions and they don't want to tell you or anyone else anything until they have the facts. I'm sure you can understand that. As for what we can do, the best thing is for us to keep praying and know that God is watching over Jim and his men and they're doing their duty to the best of their ability. I know the waiting is hard, but for now, that's what we must do."

**Monday morning, 19 January 1942
On the main defensive line along the Culo River
on the island of Luzon, Philippines**

"Think we can hold what we got, LT?"

Jim looked at the men in front of them as the soldiers continued to dig their foxholes deeper and deeper, string barbed wire, and clean and check their machine guns and other weapons. "Yeah, but at some point, instead of defending, I'd like to be attacking. Gaining the initiative. But on the good side, I feel better now knowing our flanks aren't exposed since everybody's pinched in here good and tight along this one big long line. 'Course the Japs know right where we are. Sitting ducks for all their artillery and mortars."

Sergeant Ramsey blew some smoke from his cigarette straight up into the air as he studied the sugar cane field several hundred meters to their front. "Been studying their actions real close. Seems to me the Japs have gotten themselves into a pattern. They come at us with infantry during the day and a lot of artillery and mortar fire at night along with their phony propaganda messages by 'Tokyo Rose' to keep us awake."

After gazing out at the eight-foot tall, thick cane patches two hundred yards to their front with greater intensity, Ramsey asked, "When are we gonna cut down the cane so the Japs can't use it to get close to us? Right now, they could be right on us before we could even get a bead on 'em."

"You're right. I asked about that again this morning, but the colonel seems to think we can use the cane as cover when we attack so he wants it left alone."

"That'd be true if we ever go on the attack, but right now our biggest problem is that the Japs can use it to their advantage." Ramsey sent some tobacco juice toward the ground. "The colonel say anything about reinforcements?"

"Not a word. From what I'm hearing, we've got plenty of ammunition. The big concern, at least according to the scuttlebutt from a few at battalion, is about shortages we got for food and medical supplies."

"You think maybe that's why they put us on half rations?"

"Could be. Kind of strange that McArthur's most recent Order of the Day seemed to have a different tone."

"You mean when he wrote 'Help is on the way' and, 'We have more troops than the Japs' and, 'If we fight, we will win; if we retreat we will be destroyed.' Gotta tell you, LT, I've been in this Army way too long and seen way too many commanders saying words like that for me to believe all that crap."

Ramsey grabbed his rifle and shook it. "What I believe in is this weapon right here and those men we got here with us. I'll start believing McArthur when I see all the help he's talking about with my own eyes."

The sergeant took another pull on his cigarette as he watched the men below them with a professional eye. "Tell you something else. When I first got here a year or so ago, I wasn't too keen about mixing Filipinos in the same unit with guys like us, but I got to say, I'm glad they're on our side. While they don't have all the equipment some of our units have, they know how to fight. Ain't much quit in these guys either. They're tough and smart. And since they're fighting on their homeland, they've got all the reasons they need to fight hard."

"You're right there. Up at battalion yesterday, one of our liaison officers was making the same point."

"How so?"

"Seems a couple of days ago, one of the Filipino mess sergeants with the 88th Artillery saw one of the gun crews get wiped out by Jap artillery. He got so mad he grabbed some volunteers and tore across some open ground for a good ways to put our artillery gun back in working order. Even if only part of that is true, imagine a mess sergeant grabs some other guys near him. Races across an open field for a thousand yards or so, and figures out how to fire back at the Japs. With guys like him on our side, we got a good chance to send these guys back to Tokyo with their tails between their legs."

"This guy got a name?"

"Sergeant Calugas or something like that."

Ramsey nodded. "May try and look him up and buy him a beer if I can find one. Thanks. Reminds me, heard a story much like that yesterday. About an LT over with the 57th Infantry."

Van Ostenburg gave his NCO a quizzical look. "I don't know anything about it."

"Seems this new shave-tail lieutenant named Nininger, I believe, was assigned to an infantry unit over on the eastern side of our lines. Because his unit ain't been hit yet, this guy volunteers to fight with another infantry battalion. Turns out he was a real whirlwind, attacking Jap foxholes and snipers in the trees pretty much by himself. Kept moving forward even after he got wounded a couple times. The word is he pretty much carried the whole battle by himself for a while."

"Is he staying with the new unit or did he go back to his old one?"

"Neither one. He's dead. When they found him near where they last saw him, he was lying next to a Jap officer and two Jap soldiers. All dead."

Jim stared straight ahead. *Could I do that? Attack ahead of the others?*

44

Lead the way no matter what the cost? Could I be such a man? Where do we get such men? Now if MacArthur can just get us the supplies we need, maybe we can turn the tables on Imperial Japanese's finest. Got to. Otherwise...

Monday evening, 19 January 1942
The Van Ostenburg home, Grand Rapids, Michigan

It had been a long day for Ben as he finally made it home and came in the front door. It was almost 9 PM. Unlike many other days when he stayed at the RCA store to fill orders for his customers or to repair radios others required, his tardiness this night came from attending his first meeting as the newest member of the Grand Rapids Ration Board. Unexpectedly, the four-hour marathon barely scratched the surface of the challenges before them.

Margaret met him at the door. "Why are you so late, Ben? I know this was your first meeting, but will all of them last this long?"

"Well, tonight was about one particular issue. It was all about tires, my dear. Tires."

"I don't understand. What do you mean, 'tires'? Why are they a worry based on everything else that is going on?"

"Well, I confess the subject caught me unawares as well until our local chairman, Mr. Berger, briefed us. Seems that with the Japanese now sweeping through Southeast Asia, there is either now, or soon will be, a great slowdown in the production of tires since we don't grow any rubber in our country. Seems that rubber is best grown in those places the Japanese now hold."

"So what does that mean to us?"

"Tire manufacturing will be greatly reduced and so the entire automobile industry has been ordered to end all civilian sales. This also ties into an order that the entire auto industry will soon be ordered to stop making new cars so the production lines of the big manufacturers near Detroit can be converted to making military equipment: tanks, trucks, airplanes, weapons, and other equipment. And it falls to the ration boards across the country to make decisions on who should get whatever new cars still remain at local car dealerships."

Margaret looked at her husband as she began to grasp the strain decisions like this would mean to daily life for the country as a whole. "So what did you and the others decide to do?"

"That's why the meeting was so long. Before I tell you, please understand you're not to utter a word about this to anyone."

"Yes, I understand. Of course. Go ahead."

"Our first thoughts are that the cars now in stock should go to clergy and doctors and the police forces. Then, if there are any cars left, they would go to others who can show a real need. As you can imagine a need from one man's perspective will be far different from someone else's. No doubt we're going to make some folks unhappy, but that's the way it is. The country must understand we are at war. And it will affect every aspect of our lives. And I'm sure this is just the first of many sacrifices we're all going to be asked to make."

Margaret went over to the window, staring out at some larger snowflakes coming down; the predicted heavy weather arriving as expected. "Will people be allowed to buy radios? What about your business?"

"At some point, I suspect the answer to your first question will be no, because all the materials used to build a civilian radio are the same materials required to build military radios. Having said that, I think we'll be all right because there will then be a greater reliance on keeping the radios our customers already have well-maintained. But quite frankly, I can't worry much about that right now. All of us have to consider what's best for the country as a whole, and not what it may mean to our individual businesses."

He glanced at his wife as he watched the tears roll down her cheeks. "We'll be all right. We've been through tough times before."

"I know that. I'm not worried about what you're talking about."

"What is it then?"

The woman Ben loved dearly stepped over to the big front window as the snow fell with more intensity. "Jay and Paul finished up their enlistment paperwork today. They are waiting for you upstairs. They have a special request of you."

"What request is that?"

"They would like you to be present when they enlist tomorrow."

Ben held his dear wife close as her tears continued to flow. There was little he could say as he, too, felt her concerns and her fears. Yet, pride swelled his heart. His thoughts ran to some words he heard once. "The cost of freedom is never cheap."

As his head hit his pillow later that night, he remembered the day he enlisted in the United States Army. It was a proud day. A day of excitement. And a day when he asked himself, *Will I measure up? Will I make my family proud?*

In his heart, he knew Jay and Paul were now asking themselves those same questions. *Of course I'll go with them tomorrow. And maybe, just maybe, I will be able to give them their oaths of enlistment. What an honor that would be!*

CHAPTER FOUR

"WHOSE BROAD STRIPES AND BRIGHT STARS"

World and National Events between 20 January and 3 July 1942

The world conflict during the first half of this period favors the Axis powers as German U-boats concentrate on attacking Allied shipping and the German land forces capture the Libyan port of Tobruk while consolidating their gains in Western Europe. In the Pacific theater, the Japanese seize Singapore, large portions of Burma, and the Philippine Islands, which leads to the Bataan Death March. Despite these Axis advances, the United States and her allies begin to strike back. In April, U.S. B-25 bombers are launched from a Navy aircraft carrier, delivering a psychological blow to the Japanese homeland when they bomb Tokyo. In May and June, United States and Japanese naval forces clash at the Battles of the Coral Sea and Midway, the second battle, a clear United States victory.

President Roosevelt submits a budget request to Congress for $59 billion while using an executive order to move 120,000 Japanese Americans to internment camps. In June, Roosevelt and Prime Minister Winston Churchill meet to discuss Operation TORCH, the invasion of French North Africa. They also discuss the possibility of sharing information about atomic research.

Saturday, 4 July 1942, Camp O'Donnell
on the island of Luzon, Philippines

Jim Van Ostenburg stared at the guard post one hundred yards to his left. Today it was manned by *The Cobra*, the nickname earned by the guard because of how he lashed out at the prisoners without excuse, peering at them with cold death in his eyes. It had been this way ever since the Japanese captured so many American and Filipino soldiers at the Bataan Peninsula, their hordes sweeping over them through the sugar cane Jim and others had warned their senior commanders about. While almost all the other guards exhibited a similar maliciousness, *The Cobra*, to Jim's way of thinking, was in a class by himself: his brutal and violent nature seemed limitless. *Is this what the Devil looks like in the flesh?*

As though *The Cobra* read the lieutenant's mind, the guard left his position and began to beat one of the other prisoners nearest him for no apparent reason. During the beating, the guard looked in Jim's direction sneering at him as if to say *Watch this, you soft American. I'm on the prowl and I'll strike you anytime, anywhere I want and there is nothing, nothing you can do about it. And when I do, I'll break your left wrist, just like I broke the right one.*

"Jim, you say something?" the man who sat next to him on the dry, hard ground in the shade of several scrawny palm trees asked. It had been another in a long line of scorching days of digging through the hard dirt and rocks, only to carry their bounty in large wooden buckets about a hundred yards to the site where their captors wanted to build a new road to maintain their fragile supply line.

"Yeah. Was just muttering to myself. Was thinking that *The Cobra* must be kin to the Devil himself, walking among us, beating and killing our men and the Filipinos for no reason. Truly a heinous, wicked creature."

"Know what you mean. But he's not the only one. Seen some of the others like *The Spider* and *The Maniac* do the same thing he does, preying on the sick and the weak every chance they get. Is *The Cobra* the one who cracked your wrist?"

Jim looked about at some of the other men who, like him, were trying to escape the heat for as long as they could. "Yeah, sure is. I had stopped to help one of my soldiers keep pace on the march here when he whacked me good and hard with his rifle butt. Heard the bone crack. Guess I'm lucky. Seems to be healing OK. Just got to keep it wrapped tight all the time."

"Good idea. Heard one of our colonels say the other day that they figure as many as ten thousand died on the march. Don't know who was doing the counting but I have no reason, from what I saw, to question that number. They showed no mercy to anyone. Seems to me the Filipinos got the worst of it. Guess the Japs figured since they are Orientals like them, they should be backing them and not us."

Jim watched the Japanese guard take a drink of water, that life-giving fluid that was in plentiful supply for the guards, but not for the ones they guarded. "You're probably right there. I know I didn't see any signs of what I'd call mercy from any of 'em during the march."

The lieutenant thought of the march once more. "Saw one of the Jap soldiers whack my platoon sergeant's head off with his sword simply because Ramsey stopped to help another man back to his feet. Never saw it coming. The Jap gave no warning. He just walked up to Ramsey, drew his sword, shouted something I couldn't understand, and it was over."

Jim shifted his eyes about, trying to spot *The Cobra*. "Then a few minutes later I saw another one of them bayonet a Filipino soldier for no apparent reason. Just walked up behind him and stabbed him over and over like we practiced on the cloth dummies at the bayonet assault course back at Fort Benning. Unbelievable cruelty. Any idea what causes these animals to act like that? No remorse. No mercy. If I make it to one hundred, I don't think I'll ever forget it."

Chaplain Ken Thomas sat quietly, knowing it was his job, for however long this indescribable ordeal would last, to demonstrate God's love to all around him. He knew intellectually that God's love was meant for all mankind, not just for his fellow Americans, but to the Japanese as well. His mind turned Van Ostenburg's question over and over, knowing that deep in his heart it was hard to find the love he knew he should feel as a Christian. *The Japs have put us through hell since we surrendered at Bataan. The march of 60 to 70,000 of us, sixty miles or so, with beatings and murders nearly every step of the way. Truly a death march — the Bataan Death March. Then the short miserable train ride for those who survived the march wasn't much better. Packed in rail cars like sardines in a can, crunched together so tight, you could barely take a breath, all so we could end up in this camp of never-ending misery.*

Thomas looked at the jungle around them, thinking of how, if he lived through this experience, he could describe Camp O'Donnell. *No running water. A small cup or two of rice every day for food. No medical care here worthy of the name. No escape from the oppressive tropical heat. Huge biting flies swarming from the slit trenches that surround us. Men dying every day from malaria or dysentery or beriberi or some other unknown, unnamed disease. And now with those who surrendered at Corregidor joining us, our numbers have swelled, making these conditions even more intolerable. Could it be God is showing more mercy to those who died than to those of us who remain alive? How long must we suffer, Oh Lord? How long?*

"Read somewhere that Japanese military thinking is based on the bushido code. And their ultimate warriors are the *Samurai*. Part of that philosophy is that they see surrender as a form of weakness, an act of shame. So if they get cornered, they're more inclined to commit suicide, hara-kiri they call it, instead of surrendering. Not sure if that explains it, except to say that because we surrendered, to their way of thinking, they view us as one of the lowest life forms because we gave up. We have not earned respect in their eyes because we didn't fight to the death."

But before either man could think more about that question, *The Cobra* suddenly appeared over them, kicking both men as hard as he could, like a soccer player trying to strike the ball past an opposing goalie to score the winning goal. "No talk," the beast screamed as his boots slammed into them, over and over. When Jim saw that the guard was aiming at his left wrist, he twisted quickly to protect himself, taking all the blows the monster could dish out on his back and side until the soldier grew winded, tiring of his sport. Giving them a toothy grin, the man mockingly bowed before he walked back to his guard post, a satisfied smile on his face.

With the threat now gone, Jim slowly sat up, though the pain in his body signaled that the kicks had struck several vulnerable areas. He looked about as he whispered, "Because of stuff like that, some guys are talking about trying to escape. A few are even starting to horde what food they can. They're figuring it would be best to try and get away while they've still got some stamina. You hearing anything like that?"

Thomas straightened up a little as he rubbed some of the new bruises on his thighs and calves. "Yeah. Some talk here and there. Lot of obstacles to deal with. No maps. Jungle and swamps all around. Hard for any round-eyes like us to hide. And you heard what the Jap commander said. 'If one man escapes, ten will die in his place.' At first I didn't believe him. But now, after all I've seen, I think they'd do just that. You thinking about making a break for it?"

"Giving it some serious thought. As an Infantryman, I probably got a better chance than most. Problem is just what you said. I don't want the deaths of ten men on my conscience."

Late afternoon, Saturday, 4 July 1942
Castlewellan, Northern Ireland

After another long week of training, traversing the hills of the emerald countryside around Castlewellan, a modest-sized town centered in County Down, Northern Ireland, near the Irish Sea, Jay and the rest of his crew appreciated some time off. With their almost new M4 Sherman tank safely guarded in the company laager area several miles north of the town, the crew had earned the right to enjoy some of the dry, stout Guinness beer brewed in this part of the world. Like the majority of the tank crews of Combat Command "B," 13th Armored Regiment, 1st Armored Division, Jay's crew had been on the go for the last five months.

Edger Jones, the driver, from Red Lion, Pennsylvania, was the first to speak after downing his second glass of beer as another of the delightful young lasses of Castlewellan walked by on the wide main street in front of the little tavern where the men sat. "You know when this war is over, I could see coming back here and renewing some acquaintances with some of these lovely young ladies. What a beautiful spot. Reminds me a lot of Amish country where I grew up."

The crew's gunner, Maurice Robbins, hailed from Beloit, Wisconsin. The most robust member in the crew at over six feet tall, he grunted, "You got a point there, Jonesy, but you know, we've got a lot more places to see before this war is over. So far, we've trained in the winter cold at Fort Knox, then two months at Fort Dix, and now we're in the land of the leprechauns, and we ain't seen any war yet. We've got to be getting' close, right Sarge?"

Jay Van Ostenburg took a big swig of his beer. "Yeah, you're right. We're gettin' closer with every move." He smiled, "Got to say, of the places we've seen so far, getting that thirty-six hour pass in New York City when we were at Dix was the best."

Jones grinned. "Oh yeah, you're right about that. What an unforgettable city. I was still drunk when we boarded the *Queen Mary*. Took me two days to sober up. Don't know how fast we were going, but that ship was hauling butt. No way any German sub could've gotten us."

"It was a fast ride all right," Robbins grinned. "One of the crew told me we were doing thirty knots, close to thirty-five miles an hour. Anyway, that's in the past. Now after six weeks of all this training on our new tank, I'm ready to get us some Germans. Where do you think we'll go next, Sarge? Maybe North Africa to help out the Brits?"

The tank commander took another sip of his beer to consider his response as he thought of some of the bits of information he had picked in the past week. "Right now, nobody's saying much, but I figure we'll hear something soon. To me, no matter where they send us, we still got a job to do. And as best we can, I want us all to go home in one piece."

Russell Brodie, their loader, whose freckles and inability to grow anything close to whiskers marked him as the youngest man in their crew, piped up in his western North Carolina twang. "You know, Sarge, I think we're ready. You've been pushing us hard, real hard, and to tell you the truth, we appreciate it. We've all been cross-trained in everything: the guns, how to drive the tank, how to maintain all the gear. Plus we got the best gunnery scores in the whole outfit. We know we're the best."

"Brodie, you've had too much to drink, but you're right in what you're saying," uttered Robbins. "Sarge, we all heard what the colonel said last night. 'Sergeant Van Ostenburg, this is the best tank crew in the outfit.' We know he's right. We believe in you, so when we meet up with those Krauts, we'll take those guys apart just like we do back home when we're shooting an eight-point buck. Just a question of where and when."

Despite all their praises ringing in his ears, Jay's mind harkened back to all the events of the past five months. *My father administering the oath of enlistment to my brother and me. An early promotion to Sergeant.*

Responsible for this tank crew. In one of the first units to deploy to Europe to get ready for whatever is to come next. It's exciting, yet scary at the same time. Now here I sit, experiencing all this at twenty, the oldest man in this crew.

"All right. Enough of this. Like I said, no general or colonel has pulled me aside and given me any secret plans about where we're going next. No reason to get too impatient. Our time will come soon enough. So for now, let's keep making every minute count and keep getting better. By the way, where's McIntosh? Anybody seen him?"

"Saw him walking around the town square with another redhead a little while ago. The man may be short and skinny, but for some reason which I can't figure out, he attracts girls like flies to honey. Wish I had whatever he has. Girls just can't keep their hands off him," lamented Jones.

After finishing off his Guinness, Jay threw some money on the table as he stood up. "Next round's on me. When any of you see him, make sure he doesn't get so preoccupied with his current conquest that he forgets our training tomorrow afternoon after church time. Gonna practice some more on our firing procedures. We got eighty rounds in that tank of ours and I want make sure each one hits what we're aiming at. Understand?"

"Yeah, we got it."

"Good. I'll see you all later back at camp."

Robbins sipped his beer in silence as he watched Jay saunter up the street. *Eighty rounds. Got to make every one of them count. I'm the gunner. These guys are counting on me to hit what we're aiming at. Am I good enough? Lord, please don't let me fail these men, my brothers. Their lives are in my hands, just like my life is in theirs.*

****

Jay took the longer route back to their bivouac area, strolling around the northwestern side of the town where he could gaze down on the Irish Sea some five miles away. While there was much to attract his eye, such as the Arboretum built in 1740, the Scottish castle constructed in 1856, or the pristine body of water that shared the town's name, Castlewellan Lake, his focus was on the events to come.

Upon reaching the unit area, he sought out his company commander, Captain Gary Linton. Finding the man relaxing outside the mess hall tent reading a book, Jay saluted as he approached the officer. "Sir, you got a few minutes? Got something that's been bothering me."

Linton, a thin, shallow-faced twenty-four-year-old, had been in tanks for almost three years after earning his commission through the Reserve Officer Training Corps program at Princeton University. He looked up at the sergeant, whom almost everyone considered his best tank commander, and casually retuned the salute. "Sure. What's up? Some issues with one of your soldiers?"

"No, sir. Nothing like that. My crew is solid. Got a thought about some tactics for when we meet the Germans."

Linton grinned. "Now we don't know that for sure, but just for discussion purposes, let's say you're right. What are you talking about?"

"I've been doing some studying, comparing our tanks with everything I can find out about theirs and I've got a few ideas I thought you might want to think about."

"All right, let's hear it."

"Well, sir, from what I can tell, their Panzer IIIs outgun us, and because their tank is not as tall as ours, and their gun sits lower on the chassis, they can stay hull down in some places so low, we might not even be able to see them until it's too late, which means they'll have a major advantage. On the other hand, we have the advantage when it comes to speed and maneuverability."

"Okay. I'm following you. Go on."

"And, because of the angle of the armor on their turrets, it'll be tough for us to get a kill with a head-on shot even if we see 'em first. So, the bottom line here is that if they can get accurate shots off at us first, the probability that we'll get lit up like a 'Ronson,' you know — the cigarette lighter that flames up quickly — is pretty high."

"So, if I'm reading you right, you think we're in trouble in a tank fight. But we've got a lot on our side. Our tanks can move thirty miles an hour cross-country to their twenty. We've got four guns on the M4: the seventy-five millimeter main gun, one fifty caliber and two thirty caliber machine guns. Our gyroscope sights give us the ability to hit them at twelve hundred yards. While the Panzers' guns are a bit bigger than ours like you said, and they have a lower profile, our tanks are easier to maintain, making them more dependable. And we outweigh them by five tons. So far, I haven't heard anything about any new tactics. What new tactics are you talking about?" The testiness in Linton's voice was hard to miss.

Jay stared at Linton. "Okay, sir. Here it is. Seems to me that when we go up against the Panzers, we might want to take advantage of our maneuverability to hit them from the flank or maybe the rear. If we try and attack them straight on and they're in hull down positions, they'll flame us up before we can even get off one good shot. So I was wondering if maybe we should practice some maneuvers that would allow us to take advantage of our mobility so we can get behind the Krauts. Just thought it might be something for us to consider."

Linton took time to fish a cigarette from his pocket and lit it. "How long you been in tanks?"

"About six, seven months, sir."

"So you think in that time, you've discovered more about all this tank warfare business than those of us who have been doing this for several years?"

"I didn't say I knew more, sir. I just thought we might want to consider other tactics besides a frontal attack every time. Sort of a change of pace. Maybe using our ability to move faster to take advantage of our maneuverability and hit the Panzers where they're most vulnerable, on their flanks and rear."

Linton gazed at Jay for a long time before he announced, "I got it, Sergeant. Thanks for your advice. I'll give it some thought. You're dismissed."

After Jay left, Linton smoked his cigarette down to the nub as he watched some dark rain clouds began to roll their way from over the hills to his west, turning over in his mind Van Ostenburg's comments. While his Princeton ROTC unit normally graduated men into the Field Artillery, his father pulled a few strings to meet his son's desire to join the up-and-coming tank corps, fulfilling a dream the young man had: to lead a tank unit into combat like the German blitzkrieg he had seen on the newsreels. To charge forward with speed and daring, giving the enemy no time to react. Rolling over the enemy with audacity and dash and ruthless abandon.

Linton felt the first drops of rain hit his face as he mumbled to himself. *We are the tank corps, by God. We charge like the horse soldiers of old. We face the enemy man to man, tank to tank. We don't tiptoe around to the enemy's flank or their rear, sneaking around like some infantryman. We hit the enemy hard, like a bulldozer. We bloody his nose from the front like a sledgehammer. And now this sergeant, with no real experience to speak of, is lecturing me about tank tactics? Who does he think he is? Flank shots! Not my unit. That's not how we do it in my tank corps.*

Saturday, 4 July 1942
The Van Ostenburg home, Grand Rapids, Michigan

"Those look good, Margaret."

The woman gave a quick smile as she inspected their front window, checking the lines once more to make sure they were straight and the spacing was correct. As Ben said, all three Blue stars were in perfect alignment, dress right dress. She continued to stare at the stars before commenting, "As a mother, I'm proud of our sons, but I can't help but be scared at the same time. It's a different feeling from when you went to war."

She inspected the stars once more, a habit the couple had gotten in since these stars first occupied a prominent place on the front window of their home a month ago. Clutching her husband's hands, Margaret added quietly, "I know they're doing the right thing wherever they are. They are good men." *Oh Lord, I fear soon two more stars will join these. Please keep my boys in your loving hands. Help me to keep the faith. Please help me to trust you.*

"Yes, they are, Margaret. We raised them well." Ben paused for a long moment as he stared into space. "If you don't mind, I think I'll stretch my legs some and clear my head before the others get here for the picnic. You have time to go with me?"

"I'd like to, but there are still a few things that need tending. You go ahead."

"All right. I'll be back in a half hour or so." And without another word, he stepped off the front porch into the bright sunshine. He looked back at the front window once more. *We'll be adding two more stars soon. Can't hold the two youngest ones back. Truth is I'm not sure I want to. Yes, while I will fear for their safety, I don't want them to miss the chance to serve their country.*

For a change, he took a different route this day, one he had not taken in a number of weeks. While he knew many of the families on this street, it was not one he traversed often. As he walked, he noted the number of windows displaying one, two, or three Blue stars. But the two stars that caught his attention were Gold.

Ben knew the stories of the families who lived in the two houses. John Vandervoot and Henry De Young. Both strong, young men,
younger than Jim, in fact. John died at Pearl Harbor the morning of
December 7th on the battleship *USS Oklahoma,* one of 429 men of that
crew who perished when that great vessel capsized after two Japanese
torpedoes struck her side. And Henry. He was one of the twenty-three
Marines killed on December 8th, the first day of the Japanese aerial
bombing attack on Wake Island, the same day the Japanese began their
air attack on the Philippines. By all reports, in both cases, the Japanese
attacks caught the American units sleeping at the switch. *While these
families must be proud of their son's sacrifice, they must have questions. Why
weren't our men ready? Why wasn't there adequate warning? Will there be
an investigation? What will I be feeling if one of our Blue stars changes to
Gold? How would I feel if we received a telegram from the Secretary of the
Navy or Secretary of the Army or we saw a military car stop in front of our
house one day? And Margaret? Her heart can only bear so much.*

As he stared at those symbols of sacrifice once more, Ben prayed.
*Lord, you know my struggle. It's been over six months and not a word about
Jim. Like Betty, we keep sending letters and the Red Cross packages, but
we've heard nothing. Rumors about Bataan are everywhere. We pray he and
the others with him are alive. We pray he is healthy. And if he is dead, please
let us know soon. We are a strong family, Lord, but the waiting, the unknown of it all, weighs heavy.*

Almost like a robot, Ben kept a slow, steady pace though his mind
raced. *Paul's in Florida completing his training. What about Jay? His last
letter hinted that his unit would be leaving for Ireland, but we've heard
nothing for months. Must be there by now. I understand the need for security,
but as a father, I want to know something. Since he's in tanks, he and his
men will probably go against Rommel in North Africa. And if he does, with
all this censorship, it may be months before we know anything. Timothy and
Michael are getting closer and closer to following their brothers. Can't stop*

these boys from feeling that way. I'm proud of them. Must stay strong for Margaret for whatever comes.

Saturday afternoon, 4 July 1942
Boca Raton, Florida

Paul watched the undersized waves break onto the beach for the umpteenth time, the relatively calm surf depositing one small splash after another on the shallow shore. The well-endowed blond who lay next to him on their blanket sat up. "Looks like you're a thousand miles away, soldier boy. What you thinking about? You haven't lost interest in me yet, have you?"

The newly-promoted Army Air Corps sergeant shook his head. "No, nothing like that. It's been a great day. The beach. The warm sun. The picnic. And especially being here with you. It's just... it's just I was thinking about my brothers overseas, especially the older one. My family hasn't heard anything about him in a long time. Thinking he'd like a day like this instead of whatever he must be going through."

The young woman — really just a girl two years younger than Paul — kicked idly at the sand in front of her, saying nothing for a long time. "I guess I try and keep as much of all this war stuff in the background as I can. I don't have any brothers, and while a lot of boys around here have joined up, the reality of the war hasn't hit me personally yet, except for all this rationing stuff, of course. I'm just hoping it will all be over soon."

The girl turned on her side and asked, "I know you're going to some school here, and I was wondering, what are they teaching you anyway?"

Paul drew a deep breath. This girl next to him was another in a series he had spent time fancying up to since he arrived in the Boca area a few months ago after finishing basic training, the small town occupying a quiet piece of land along the Atlantic Ocean about half-way between

West Palm Beach and Miami. Most of the girls he had met, while quite appealing in their own way, seemed to be in some state of denial and had no real understanding about how serious the world situation had become. *At least this one asked a good question.*

"In a nutshell, I'll by flying in transport airplanes moving supplies from one place to another and my job is make sure we stay in contact with all the ground elements involved. That involves using radios, direction finders, and some other gear on the aircraft."

The blond sighed, "OK, I was just wondering. Sounds pretty interesting. I thought you might be a pilot or something like that."

"No, sorry to disappoint you." *If I'm going to have any serious relationship with any girl while I'm here, I need to look for one with brains who is also pleasing on the eyes. No question this one today gets high marks on looks, but she falls short in the other category.*

He took a quick look around at the deserted beach. *But since I'm here and we're on a deserted part of the beach, it would be silly to not take advantage of the situation...* Afterward, Paul's thoughts turned to Jim and Jay. *Keep the faith, brothers. Keep the faith. I'll be joining you overseas soon. Only got another fifteen weeks to finish my training, pin on my wings, and head to the war somewhere.*

He looked around once more to make sure he and his companion remained alone before he rolled over once more to enjoy the warm sun and the warm body next to him. *Twenty years old is a great age. Better enjoy this while I can.*

Late afternoon, Saturday, 4 July 1942
The Van Ostenburg home, Grand Rapids, Michigan

"Mrs. Van, thank you for inviting me to the family picnic. I always feel closer to Jim whenever I'm here," Betty said as her eyes welled up.

"I know, dear. I know. We'll hear something soon. I know we will."

"I hope so. I just want to know he's all right. I keep sending letters and packages like the Red Cross instructed us to do, but... but the not knowing is the toughest thing of all."

Margaret tried to give Betty an encouraging smile. "When Ben was overseas in France, even in the best of times mail was always slow. Didn't hear from him for three or four months at a time, so I know exactly what you are going through. It's easy to say, but my advice is for all of us to keep praying."

Betty looked at her mother-in-law. "I will. I will. Thank you."

****

Ben and his brother watched the stars begin to make their presence known, twinkling in the dark eastern sky, more of them becoming visible with each turn of the head. "With such a peaceful sky above, it's hard to believe there's a war going on."

"You're right, Bud. But, on the other hand, on a night like this with all these stars above us, I can't help but think that even in the midst of all the turmoil, God has everything under control. So while our struggles could overwhelm us, maybe we should just look up and remind ourselves who's really in charge."

"I suppose you're right. You mentioned struggles. Anything going on?"

"Just the normal things. Those of us on the Ration Board hear complaints every day from one group or another, each one wanting an exception for this or for that. And because we issue few exemptions, most folks understand, but there are a few I'd like to take to the woodshed."

Bud chuckled. "I can believe that, although I think most everyone is coming around. Everybody's got ration cards now and they're learning how to deal with that. A lot of good, old-fashioned horse trading going around some, too. Those I talk to seem to be trying to make a game out of collecting scrap metal, tin, and rubber, all with an understanding it's for the war effort in one way or the other. Heard about something the other day I wanted to ask you about."

Ben closed his eyes for a moment. "And what would that be?"

"Is it true that we'll even be collecting milkweed soon?"

"Yep. True enough. Seems when the milkweed pods dry out in the fall, scientists have figured out that since they're coated with wax, they become buoyant and waterproof, and so those pods will be used in life vests. So, in the not-too-distant future, we'll be having contests to see who can collect the most milkweed pods. Surprised me too when I heard about it, but that's what we'll be doing."

"Well I'll be. What will they think of next?"

"Hard to say, but I'm sure eventually another scientist will make another discovery we can take advantage of. Constraints on coffee, sugar, and foodstuffs will continue. And without question, with many families growing their own 'Victory Gardens,' that has had some real pluses. And Spam seems to be catching on. At least its meat, even if you can't identify everything in it. Even got Margaret trying out a few different ways to cook it. Pretty good even if I do say so myself."

"You know, Ben, the one benefit of all this rationing has been for me to get more exercise. With gas in short supply, I'm either walking to places like church or I'm riding a bike again like when I was a kid. Lost about ten pounds in the last two months."

"Bud, you may have something there. We could call it 'The Benefits of Rationing.' But you know we already have a pretty good slogan already."

"Yeah, what's that?"

Ben smiled. "It's simple but catchy. 'Use it up, wear it out, make it do, or do without.' But I'll run your idea by the Rationing Board at our next meeting. We're always looking for good ideas. Thanks."

"No problem."

"Oh, before I forget, in the next few weeks, I'll be appointed to one of the draft boards. Seems they've had a few openings because some others have had health issues, and because of my time overseas, they've asked me to fill in. Figured I'd mention that to you because if they have more openings, I'm going to nominate you since you've had experience wearing Army green. You'd be a good man for that."

"That's fine with me. Would be a good way to serve since I'm too old to pull a lanyard on an artillery piece. Yeah, go ahead. Put my name in."

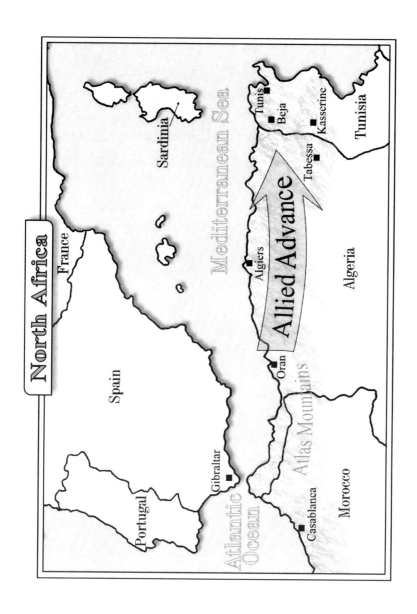

CHAPTER FIVE

"THRU THE PERILOUS FIGHT"

World and National Events between
5 July and 23 December 1942

THE ALLIED FORCES PUSH BACK GERMANY AND JAPAN ON SEVERAL fronts. While the German advance into Russia generally favored the attacker, the depth of the Russian landscape takes its toll on the advancing German forces. In North Africa, British forces launch a major offensive against the Germans in October at the Battle of El Alamein, which is then followed by Operation TORCH—Allied troops landing in western North Africa in an effort to pinch the Germans between the two Allied armies. In the Pacific theater, United States Marines land on Guadalcanal in the Solomon Islands, signaling the opening of what became known as the island hopping campaign.

On the home front, the citizens of the United States grapple with the sacrifices required to win the war, as Congress authorizes the President to control wages and agricultural prices. And in great secrecy, President Roosevelt decides the United States would develop an atomic bomb without the assistance of England.

Christmas Eve, Thursday, 24 December 1942
On a hilltop overlooking the Medierda Valley, thirty miles west of
Tunis, Tunisia, North Africa

While Jay had attended only a few of the division chaplain's services in the past month, it was clear that the man spoke from the heart to the large gathering of soldiers about the meaning of Christmas. The site chosen for the celebration was atop one of the large rocky slopes in the Atlas Mountain chain that dominated the North African landscape overlooking the Mediterranean Sea to the north. While he had no way of knowing about all the religious affiliations and faiths represented in the group of more than two hundred men who made their way to the precipice, Jay sensed there was almost an equal mix of those who learned in their childhood what Christmas was all about and those who struggled to find its meaning amidst all the chaos and mayhem they had experienced these past two months.

Following the service as Jay and his gunner, Maurice Robbins, walked down the rock-strewn trail, working their way around several large rock outcroppings toward their tank's position several thousand yards away, a cool wind accompanied them every step of the way.

Jay stopped for a moment to gaze at the eastern sky. "Every night I look up at those stars above us, I wonder how this will end. Know what I mean?"

"Sure do. Not many days have gone our way."

"Yeah, that's true... Whoa! You see that?"

"See what?"

"That shooting star. Moving fast southeast to northwest."

"OK, I see it. Oops... Gone now. You think maybe it was a star like that maybe the wise men saw that the chaplain was talking about tonight?" Robbins asked in a reverent tone. "You know I've heard that story the chaplain told us many times before, but tonight the wise men, the star in the east, the manger, became much more real to me."

Jay Van Ostenburg kept his eyes on the night sky. "Yeah. I suspect that's true for a lot of the guys on that hilltop tonight."

Before either man could say another word, a different flash of light caught their attention. They then heard a deep, distant rumble well to the southeast a few seconds later. "Kraut artillery. Reminds me, I want you to take our new guy, Batten, and make him your personal project. Get him off to the side and get him trained up fast about the difference between what our weapons and their weapons sound like. Every weapon. Tanks. Artillery. Machine guns. Airplanes. Everything. Don't know when, but the word is the bigwigs are ginning up another huge operation — least that's what Captain Reynolds was saying this morning. I'm hoping it's just officer talk, but you never know. Now that we've been resupplied and we got a bunch of replacements like Batten, it wouldn't surprise me if we move out soon. You hearing any scuttlebutt?"

"Nah, nothing. And because we ain't hearing anything, that's a sure sign something's brewing. I'd lay some good money on that. Speaking of our new CO, what do you think about him?"

"He's still learning, but at least he listens. Asks a lot of questions. And he doesn't act like he knows everything. Seems like that's a good thing to me."

As the two men continued their hike down the hill, Jay thought about the last two months. *Traveling from the Emerald Island in late October on those stinking, crowded ships and landing east of Oran, Algeria. Catching hell from the Germans when we got into the fight. Their years of combat experience showing itself very quickly. Two of my crew blown to bits. Watching men, ours and theirs alike, burned beyond recognition inside their steel coffins. Seeing steel hulks being split wide open in a flash by screeching high-velocity rounds that strike just the right spot. Hearing the tortured screams of those inside that stopped only when they take their last breath. Oh God, I pray you will take the sights and sounds and smells of all this away from me.*

71

Robbins interrupted his thoughts. "You ever get that letter sent? You know the one to Brodie's parents?"

"No, not yet. Only been a couple of weeks. I'll try and get to it today. Guess I've been struggling with what to say and how to say it." He glanced up the stars once again. *How do you tell a mother or a father that their son was burned to death in a tank and that the rest of us got out alive?*

"I know I've got to write it. I could tell you I've just been searching for the right words, but the truth is I'm stalling, hoping I'll get so busy I won't have time to get to it."

Robbins, the man a few months younger than Jay, made no further comment as they crested the last small hill that led down to their position. Their tank, nicknamed *Glorious Glenda* for no particular reason, sat nestled in a small protective shelter of some large boulders next to the platoon's other three M4 Shermans.

When they reached *Glenda*, Robbins looked at his friend. "I can understand why you're delaying writing that letter. It's times like these when I'm glad you're the tank commander and not me. Not sure what or how I'd write it. But I'll tell you this. It was you who pulled me and Jones out of that inferno that used to be our tank and were turning back to get Brodie out when that thing blew up."

"Yeah, but..."

"No, 'Yeah buts,' Jay. Like I told the officers who asked, you did all you could do to get him out alive. And the higher-ups must have agreed with me since they pinned that red, white, and blue Silver Star on you. Not every day somebody gets that. What did the colonel say when he pinned it on you? 'For action in combat well above the call of duty.' I know I won't forget what you did. If you hadn't stuck your neck out for Jones and me, you'd have been listening to Chaplain Cook's message by yourself tonight. You saved our butts and we owe you."

Robbins paused to make sure Jay was listening. "You are a good man, Jay Van Ostenburg. Whatever you end up telling Brodie's parents, I'm sure it'll bring some comfort to them."

Jay stood still, staring at the first streaks of daylight in the east. After a long pause, he nodded. "Thanks. I'll get the letter written today." He then gave his crewman a quick smile. "You just get Batten squared away. We need him to be ready, best as we can, to take on whatever comes our way. Oh, and lest I forget, Merry Christmas."

****

Later that day, Jay wrote two letters, the first to Brodie's parents and the other to his father. In the second letter he penned *"... We were soft in November. Our officers were timid, unsure of themselves, too slow to react. And we paid a heavy price for it. But we're getting a little tougher every day as we become more accustomed to the brutality of war. Because we have seen so much of it, we don't fear death as much as we once did, only how it may come.*

Initially we feared the Germans because they kicked our butts so bad, but now we're giving it back to them as much as they give it to us. And because we have almost an endless amount of supplies and replacements, the tide seems to be turning in our favor. Our morale is improving as our commanders and leaders become more experienced. I know you'll understand what I'm saying here and can read between the lines..."

After sealing the letter, Jay wondered if the unit censors who checked the outgoing mail would razor out some of his words. As he thought about that, he decided to send the letter as written. The censors could do whatever they thought best. He just wanted to get some of his thoughts on paper.

Christmas Day, Friday, 25 December 1942
Camp O'Donnell, on the island of Luzon, Philippines

As soon as the outdoor worship service was over and before the sun's rays began to heat up the air too much, Jim went up to the chaplain as the others who had attended the early morning service moved toward the shady spots.

"Thanks, Chaplain. Appreciate your words. Guess I never thought of the Israelites wandering around in the desert as a Christmas message, but I can see where it fits. All things considered, God is still watching over us."

The man, who Jim judged to be about eight or nine years older, smiled. "Well, I'll tell you, Jim, it wasn't my usual Christmas message I'd give back home, but for this place and this time, it seemed to fit. I hope it'll help these guys. Not exactly the garden spot of the Pacific, but this is where God has placed us for now. In this... place."

"You almost said, 'God-forsaken,' didn't you?"

Chaplain Thomas looked about at all the starving, emaciated men for a long time before answering. "Yeah, guess I did." He then let out a deep sigh. "But something deep inside me made me realize that even in this hell-hole, God has not forgotten us, even though, I admit it takes some work at times to remember that."

Jim looked around at the small weather-beaten canvas hovels the men had lived in now for almost eight months, all their clothes now threadbare, most of the men shoeless. Nothing had been done by their captors to improve their living conditions. Their slit trenches still reeked of the diseases the men now carried deep in their loins, and the mounds of dirt that served as burial grounds gave evidence to the seventy or eighty men who died each day as they succumbed to their injuries or diseases or the acts of cruelty on the part of their Japanese tormentors.

"I think you're onto something with your message that even if we grumble about our present circumstances, God is still present. Each day I wake up and try to remember something my father told me a few years ago. He was in the Great War, his unit surrounded and running out of bullets, water, food, bandages, everything. He told me he learned that as long as you can still breathe, you've got a chance. Just got to keep fighting, because as soon as you stop, you'll lose hope, and if you lose hope, you die. I try and hold onto that thought every day."

"Your father sounds like a very wise man. I'd like to meet him some day."

"I think he'd like that." Jim looked around the camp again. "Heard you humming a few old hymns the other day as you walked around. You gonna do that again today?"

Thomas chuckled, "Yeah, that's my new thing to encourage the guys as I take my daily walk-about, as the Aussies say. And since the Japanese aren't likely to know the tunes I'm humming, I can probably get away with it for a while."

"Yeah, I can see that."

"In my last church where I was pastor before the war, the ladies of my congregation suggested, without any hesitation on their part I might add, that I confine my hymn singing to the privacy of my home. That being said, thank you for recognizing that my humming of hymns is somewhat close to the correct notes. I think today I'll focus on blessing the camp with some of the old familiar Christmas carols." He gave a wry smile. "Who knows, maybe a few of the Japs may be taken in by my melodious tenor sounds."

The chaplain surveyed his surroundings, paying particular attention of the positioning of the guards who, on this day, did not seem to be on their normal prowl through the camp, giving the POWs some small bit of freedom. "Think I'll head first over to our so-called infirmary. Even if the Japs can't provide our men any medicine for their bodies, maybe I can give our guys something for their souls. You be a blessing to some-one today, Jim. It's Christmas."

"Yeah, I'll try and do that. On a different subject, you seen *The Cobra* today?"

"No, but if I do see him, I'll give him a wide berth. Seems in the past few weeks, that beast has gotten worse instead of better. Not sure why, but... See you around Jim."

"Will do. Say, before you go, did you taste some of that food some of the guys tried to cook last night?"

Thomas laughed. "If you mean the barbequed monkey or that skinny pig that made the mistake of trying to run through camp, along with the king cobra somebody managed to kill, yes, I did. Wasn't that bad all things considered."

"You're right. Some of it anyway. Couldn't tell exactly what it was but it tasted pretty good going down. However, about a half hour later, it looked really bad coming back up. Probably wasn't cooked as long as it should have been, but since everyone is so hungry, nobody could wait. Even if it was a bit raw, it tasted better than bananas for a change."

"Suppose you're right. If I thought about it long enough, there's probably a good sermon there somewhere. Let me change the subject on you. Haven't heard you mentioning anything about trying to make a break for it. You give up the idea?"

"Not totally. While I think I might be able to make it either alone or with a few other guys trained like me, to have Japs behead, shoot, or torture some of you left behind on my account is not something I can easily put aside. Not sure I want other deaths to be on my conscience."

Thomas glanced around at some of their fellow prisoners, some of whom could barely walk. "I understand. To have someone beheaded for my desires is not something I could live with either. Thanks for telling me. You're a good man, Jim. It's my privilege to know you."

As Ken Thomas walked away, Van Ostenburg studied the man. *Yes, even as he suffers like all the rest of us, he seems to have an inner core of faith that cannot be shaken. He never stops ministering, never stops leading, never stops encouraging, no matter how tough the circumstances are around him. He's been beaten and starved like us, and yet through it all, he thinks about others first. Truly a tower of strength and humility at the same time.*

Staring into the deep jungle that held them captive perhaps even more than the guards and the barbed wire, Jim turned his thoughts toward home. *Wonder what Betty is doing today? I doubt that any word has reached her. Got to be tough. She's got to be wondering if I'm alive or dead, yet the memory of her warm embrace keeps me going every day and every night. And what about my brothers? They all talked about serving. Wonder if any of them are close? And my mother and father? Are they still alive? Will I ever see them again?*

Christmas, Friday, 25 December 1942
Chabau Army Air Corps Base, Chabau, India

"Little different from last Christmas, ain't it, Paul?

Paul nodded as he and Dave Keller, another radio operator who shared one of the sixteen spaces in their large thatched hut, walked along the side of hard-packed dirt runway at their new home. Arriving within two days of each other, the men renewed their acquaintance from communications school. After their three-week journey to India, both airmen felt the need to stretch out their travel-weary legs.

"Yeah, you could say that. Last year I was at home with three of my four brothers. My mom had the house decorated to the hilt and the food was great. I'm sure when the chow hall opens up here later today the smells won't be quite the same. And it'll be a hundred degrees instead of twenty-five with snow."

Keller, a year older than Paul, laughed as he showed off his eastern

Tennessee twang, "You got that right for sure. Don't get this kind of heat and humidity in the mountains where I come from. What are we? Ninety feet above sea level in this valley. No wonder it's hot. And the food? I'm sure it won't be anywhere close to the barbequed hog my folks are having back home today. Tell you what. After this is all over, just remember, you've got an open invitation to a great Christmas meal in Erwin, Tennessee, right on the western edge of the Smokies."

"Deal. I'll take you up on it first chance I get."

"Good. Now you said something about your brother missing from last Christmas. He in the Army Air Corps, too, or something else?"

"Infantry officer stationed in the Philippines. He was there when the Japs attacked last year. And since then, nothing. Don't know if he's dead or alive."

"That's got to be tough on your folks, not knowing."

"Yeah, it is. And on his wife. They got married just before he shipped out. Anyway, my twin brother and I enlisted back in January this year. After doing my basic training at Maxwell, I went to Boca and you know the rest."

The two continued their saunter for a few more minutes before Paul added, "Don't think I told you that just before we left Florida, I met a girl. My gut tells me she's the one. She said she'd wait for me, but you know how that goes. Lot of guys get their 'Dear John's' no matter what the girl said before they left."

"Yeah. Heard plenty of stories about some girls doing that already. Leaving their man high and dry after they leave. Well, I hope this girl waits for you." Keller looked intently at the snow-covered caps of the Himalayas well to the northeast. "What's her name?"

"Eleanor. Not only pretty, but smart, too. Brother is training to be a Field Artillery officer. She's pretty special. Volunteers to spend two nights a week looking for anything suspicious out in the Gulf Stream from one of those tall buildings along the coast south of West Palm

Beach. Told me she spotted a transport ship get torpedoed by a German sub a few months back. She called the rescue folks and they were able to save some of the crew."

"Sounds like a great girl, Paul. Hope it works out for you."

"Thanks. Me, too." The two men stopped to watch one of the base's olive-colored C-47s, whose official name was "Skytrain," though its unofficial name by those who flew it was "The Gooney Bird," taxi to the end of the runway. The pilot then revved up his plane's two big Pratt and Whitney engines as it swung around to face the long runway, the nose of the plane tilted slightly toward the sky.

Paul spoke above the sound of the engines, "We'll be taking our orientation flight in the next two or three days. I don't know about you, but I'm ready to start chalking up some missions. The sooner we get our fifty, the sooner we go home."

Keller nodded but said nothing as he thought about why they were in India. *Here we are. Part of the Air Transportation Command. Mission is ferry supplies from India over the Himalayas to Kunming, China so Chiang Kai-shek and his Chinese soldiers can take on the Japs in his country. The C-47 is a good bird. Range sixteen hundred miles. Maximum ceiling twenty-four thousand feet, carrying five tons of supplies at over two hundred miles an hour. But look at those mountains. What happens if...?*

They watched the plane gain speed as it hurtled down the runway, finally leaving the ground behind, and beginning a slow climb eastward. "How's your navigator?" asked Keller.

"Seems to be real good. Lieutenant Brown. A big guy. Twenty-two. Red mustache. Hard to miss him. Pretty good as a co-pilot, too. Went through Nav School at San Marcos Field."

"Where's that?"

"Out in the middle of nowhere Texas. Between Austin and San Antonio. Must have learned his stuff pretty good because he seemed to be right on the money on all the stops we had to make to get here.

Twenty-three in all between West Palm and here. Puerto Rico. Two along the South American coast. Ascension Island in the middle of the South Atlantic. Accra. Ghana. Khartoum. The Middle East. Karachi. And Calcutta before we followed the Brahmaputra River to get here. Gave our plane, *The Busy Bee*, a real good shake-down. About ten thousand miles or so total flying distance. You fly the same route?"

"Yep. Exactly the same. And from what everybody here is saying, now the real flying starts."

"Yeah, I heard that. Everyone who's been here for a while that I've talked to says that every flight over those mountains has the potential to be an adventure. High winds. Cold, brutal temperatures aloft. Engine and wing icing. No place to land if you get in trouble."

The two watched "The Gooney Bird" until it disappeared in a thin layer of clouds as the aircraft continued its climb, the route taking it directly over the mountain range to the east toward the fifteen thousand foot, jagged, snowcapped mountains.

"Tell you what, Dave. Let's see if the turkey and trimmings are ready. I'm hungry."

As Paul walked along next to his friend, his thoughts turned in many directions. *Well, I got what I wanted. A chance to fly. But what a dismal place this is. These people have so little. Need to write Mom and Dad and tell them I'm OK. Can't tell them everything, of course, because of the censorship rules, but I'll mention the thatched roof building and the hemp rope cots. No matter how bad that sounds, it's nothing like what the infantry goes through every day. Hope by now they've heard something about Jim. Distance-wise I'm the closest to him if he's still alive. Rumors here say the Japs are as bad as they come in dealing with their prisoners. Then there's Jay. Probably in North Africa going up against some of Rommel's boys. Guess I won't hear much about him for a while. Tim and Mike should be joining up soon. God, please be with all my brothers and Mom and Dad.*

Christmas Day, Friday, 25 December 1942
The Van Ostenburg home, Grand Rapids, Michigan

Throughout the day, Ben tried to focus on the holiness of the celebration, but without much success. Despite their traditional gathering for Christmas dinner with the family and all the smells that accompanied the traditional foods as best as they could muster through the rationing system, he could not get his mind off his sons. Jim, Jay, and Paul. *God be with you boys. God be with you.* After the family finished their meal and Ben took his customary seat in the living room, he found his heart moved again.

"Dad?"

Ben turned to see his two youngest sons standing before him. "Yes, boys, what is it?"

"Michael and I want to take a walk with you just like you've done with our brothers."

"I'm not sure what you mean, Timothy. 'Take a walk like you've done with your brothers?'"

"Come on, Dad. We know what you've done after Christmas dinner the last few years. You took the other guys for a long walk, telling them about your days in the Army. Since we're close to enlisting, we think it's time you took us for that same walk."

"You two got your minds pretty well made up about enlisting?"

"Yes, sir. We have. To do anything else would be embarrassing. We're both thinking that from everything we've heard, and knowing how we like pushing ourselves, we both know what we want to do."

"You do? And what exactly is that?"

"We want go into the infantry. And because we've been together almost every step of our lives, being twins and all, we're thinking now we'd each like to be on our own. You know, go to different units. Not join the same one."

Ben stared at each of them for a moment, both trim and sturdy like their brothers. "You tell your mother about what you two are thinking?"

"No, sir. Not yet. Figured we'd talk to you first. Shouldn't be a big surprise to her since we've been giving out a lot of hints about this for a while."

"Michael, you're just standing there. You got anything to add or is Timothy saying what's on your mind as well?"

"Tim's got it about right. We know we've got the brains to do a lot of other things. Communications, logistics, signal intelligence, stuff like that, but those don't appeal to either one of us. We want to be tested. Somewhere we can feel like we're making the biggest contribution. So the infantry seems like the best place for us. We know it'll be tough, but we're OK with that."

"You two have been watching too many newsreels. You almost sound like a recruiting poster."

"Don't mean to. Guess what we're both trying to say is that we want to be like you. We want to follow in your footsteps. Nothing more. Nothing less."

****

The early morning snow had given way to a harsh late afternoon chill, the temperature hovering close to zero as the three slowly made their way along the familiar path, each being careful to avoid the icy spots. No words passed between them until Ben asked, "When you two say you want to be infantrymen, do you have any idea what you're talking about?"

This time it was Michael who took the lead. "We're sure we don't know everything about it, but what we do know is that it is important, and if it helped you become the man you are, then that's good enough for us."

"Humph. All right, I can accept that for now, but after some sergeant rips into you for the slightest bone-head error, I don't want to hear any whining or sniveling from either of you. The infantry way of doing things will either hone a man's character or it'll expose him for the quitter that he is. I have confidence in you two that you'll turn out for the better, but just know you'll see some men who you first believed were tough enough. Then, all of the sudden, you'll see these same guys crack under pressure. They simply can't take it, and the sooner they're found out, the better it is for all concerned. Infantry training is designed to expose men like that—men who aren't mentally and physically tough enough to take it."

"Yes, sir," the two boys replied in unison.

"Since you two probably heard some of what I've told your brothers, I won't repeat myself. For now, I'll just give you a few things to ponder before you sign your names on the dotted line of those enlistment papers. Probably won't surprise you, but I'll tell you anyway."

With that, Ben started to walk a little slower, wanting to make each word count. "First, before you open your mouths too quickly, think first, because once you agree to something, anything, you have made a bond, an oath, a promise. You've heard me say it before. Let your word be your bond. Said another way — say what you mean and mean what you say. Any questions about that?"

"No, sir."

"Second, and this applies especially to infantrymen, focus on the important things and don't waste time on the small stuff. A simple example. I once had a sergeant who was more interested in making sure our boots were spit-shined than he was in making sure our rifles were clean and well-maintained. He didn't last long. He had his priorities out of order. In the infantry, we focus on the important, not the unimportant."

Ben took a few more steps before he finished. "Always treat the man on your right and your left with respect. There will be a few who don't deserve that respect and they will identify themselves quickly, but for all the others, remember you hold the lives of the man on your right and on your left in your hands, and they in turn hold your life in theirs. Don't ever forget that."

Monday, 4 January, 1943
Chabau Army Air Corps Base, Chabau, India

Paul read over the letter one more time before he put the three-cent stamp on the envelope, a purple colored one with the eagle in the middle of it with the words "Win the War" across it.

Dear Dad,

We just completed our first mission. Can't tell you the exact location we flew to, but it's well east of where I'm stationed. Know you will get some ideas when you look at a map. Airplane was full and we delivered our supplies on time. Because it was our first mission, we trailed another airplane, but from now on, we'll be making these flights on our own.

It was an exhilarating experience. To see that all we trained for, works. The two officers I fly with are professional in every way. They fly the bird and navigate to where we're going and I keep us in touch with all the bases and places we're going to and from. I'm glad to be serving here doing something important.

Please tell mom my accommodations aren't quite up to her standards in a variety of areas but we make do. Hope by now you've heard something from Jim. I trust Jay's also doing well. I'll write again soon.

Your loving son, Paul

As he closed up the letter and began to seal it, David Keller stopped by Paul's bunk. "So how was the first flight? You obviously made it back in one piece. Got to ask since we're taking our orientation flight tomorrow at first light."

Paul continued to double-check the seal on the envelope. "I remember someone telling me that as long as your number of take-offs equals the number of landings, you've had a good flight. So from that standpoint, we took off from here. We landed at Kunming. They unloaded the gasoline and food and ammunition we had in the back of the bird. We stayed on the ground for two hours as they gassed us up and then we flew back here. A total of fourteen hours."

"And?"

"I figured we missed gettin' killed only three or four times."

"You're kidding, right?"

"No. Not a bit. We flew the 'Nan' route to Kunming. Missed one of the peaks by maybe two, three hundred feet. We couldn't see the plane we were supposed to follow because after we went through a huge thunder and lightning storm in the first hour, we never him saw again until we got to Kunming. And because we found ourselves flying alone toward Kunming, Lieutenant Brown had a tough time finding the airstrip. We finally landed with about thirty minutes of gas in our tanks. Then on the return flight on the 'Oboe' route, we got lost again and had trouble landing because of the cross-winds that were zipping across the runway at thirty or forty knots. Other than that, it was a piece of cake. Our next mission is in three or four days."

Keller stared at Paul. "I guess this means you've got one mission done and another forty-nine or so to go."

"Yeah. Guess that's probably the best way to look at it. Oh, by the way, when you land at Kunming on one of their two ten-thousand-foot crushed stone runways that isn't so crushed, the Chinese cooks there will tell you that you can have fresh eggs cooked anyway you want. But don't get too excited. No matter how you want your eggs, you'll get 'em scrambled."

85

"Gotcha. See you finishing a letter. You telling the folks back home about our luxurious accommodations?"

"You mean did I tell my mom about our slit trenches that are filled to overflowing or about the chicken stew we had last night that was full of feathers and bones and a little meat or that there's little to do around here if we're not sleeping or checking our airplane to make sure it's ready to fly? Nah. Didn't tell her any of that. They've got enough to worry about. There'll be plenty of time to give them all the details of paradise when we get back home. Right now, like you said, I've got one down and forty-nine to go."

Paul stood up, stretching his weary body. "Now if you got some time, let me fill you in on what I learned about trying to communicate with the stations along the routes. Also got to get my act together on some of the load master duties. Didn't realize when I came here, I'd be doing some of that, too. Getting all those boxes first into the bird through the side doors and then everything all tied down good and tight is no easy task. And if the load starts coming loose while we're getting bounced around in-flight, I've learned to be real careful. Double-check every knot, every tie-down strap. Can't be too careful."

Keller gave Paul a weary look. "Yeah, I heard that. If something comes loose, it could ruin your whole day."

Tuesday afternoon, 5 January 1943
After the Draft Board Meeting, Grand Rapids, Michigan

"Ben, you got a minute?"

"Yes, sir. Of course," Ben said as Mr. Van Dyke guided him over to a quiet corner of the room. "Anything wrong?"

Van Dyke, a large Dutchman well over six feet tall, several years older than Ben, and like him, a veteran of the Great War, put his hand on Ben's shoulder. "Ben, I was at a meeting at the State Capital building in Lansing last week. There are some rumors that are now coming out, unsubstantiated and unconfirmed certainly, about how the Japanese are treating their prisoners of war. These reports are sketchy. They come from those who have escaped from the Japs in Malay, Hong Kong, and maybe even from the Philippines. There haven't been a great number of escapees, but there have been enough that we're starting to get a feel for how they're treating their POWs."

Ben looked at the man's face, trying to read into his words. "How bad is it?"

Van Dyke's head dropped down. "There's talk of beheadings, firing squads, maltreatment of every description. I don't have any specifics, but I thought you should know. As I hear anything of substance, anything at all, I'll let you know. I'll be praying for you and your family, Ben. Especially for Jim."

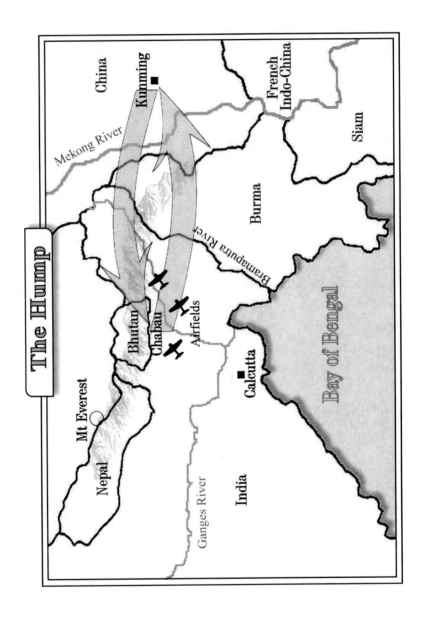

CHAPTER SIX

"O'ER THE RAMPARTS WE WATCHED"

World and National Events between 6 January and 2 July 1943

WHILE BATTLES RAGE ON ALL FRONTS, ALLIES WIN HARD-FOUGHT VICtories in North Africa against the Germans, while massive battles in Russia inflict heavy damage on both the Wehrmacht and the Red Army. In the European theater, President Roosevelt and Prime Minister Churchill give priority to invading Italy while rendering the German submarine force ineffective, and initiating Operation POINTBLANK, the strategic bombing campaign of Germany. Along with these advances, Allied leaders target 1 May 1944 as the date to invade Europe. In the Pacific, United States capture several large islands in the Solomon Island chain and renew efforts to retake New Guinea.

On the home front, Congress votes to continue with the Lend-Lease program for another year and President Roosevelt bars war contractors from racial discrimination.

Saturday, 3 July 1943
Deshon General Hospital, Butler, Pennsylvania

It was a wonderful reunion for the Van Ostenburg family, especially for

Margaret. Though the train ride from Grand Rapids to Butler, Pennsylvania, twenty-five miles north of Pittsburgh, seemed to take forever, to see her wounded son in one of the recovery wards of the large complex wearing a casual set of slacks and shirt, with no visible signs of pain and distress, was an answer to her prayers. Since the first notification arrived in late May that Jay had been wounded in action, and would be receiving treatment at Deshon Hospital prior to his release from active duty, she had feared the worst. But now seeing him and talking to him and watching him move about, she was relieved. And while Ben had hidden his concerns quite well, he, too, found it hard to contain his joy.

"So Jay, what're they telling you about when you'll be released from here? And what about dates regarding your release from active duty?"

"As I understand it, I'll be continuing physical therapy treatments for my legs for another month or so, and then I'll spend another two months here on limited duty helping other guys transition out of the service before I'm officially retired from active duty. The docs have also told me I'll be carrying some shrapnel home in my leg, but that's no big deal. Guess when you add it all up, I'll be a civilian again right around Thanksgiving time, after you tack on a month's worth of leave. In the meantime I plan on contacting Mr. Vodermark and letting him know when I'll be back ready to work again."

Ben smiled, "Well, that's good to hear, son. Matter of fact I saw him a few days ago and he was asking about you. From what he said, I know he's ready to have you back. His business seems to be growing and he indicated he's got some things he wants you to help him with. If I were you, I'd give him a call pretty quick."

"Got it, Dad. I'll try and get permission to make that long distance call next week."

Jay looked about the large ward he was in, at the other ten soldiers that lounged on the beds, some reading and others listening to several radios. "Going back to being a civilian again will be quite a change. These are good men. I will miss being around them."

"I know what you mean, son. I know what you mean. We've both been blessed to be around such men as these."

"Yeah, we have, Dad. Before I take my uniform off, I need to help some of these guys cope with what they might be facing. Some of these men lost arms and legs. And I also need to see several families of the men I served with."

"Are you two now going to talk in some Army code?" asked Margaret.

"Maybe a little bit, Mom. But you're welcome to stay."

"Jay, if I've learned nothing else from living with your father all these years, there are times when men just need some time by themselves. Knowing that you're doing so well, I'm going to take a walk outside and enjoy the sunshine while I praise God for bringing you back in one piece." She smiled as she kissed her son on the cheek. "I'll be back in about thirty minutes."

After watching Margaret walk down the hall, Ben looked at his son. "I hope you'll be lucky enough to find a woman like your mother. I have truly been blessed."

"We all have, Dad. We all have."

The two combat veterans sat quietly for a few minutes, each gathering his thoughts, before Jay opened up. "Couldn't write a lot of details in my letters because of security and all, but as you probably figured, it was a long, tough fight."

"Yeah, I assumed that from what you didn't say and what the press said and didn't say. About those families you mentioned you need to see — are these the families of those who are not coming home?"

"Yes, sir. Two families are within driving distance. They deserve to know what happened to their sons. Once I can move about better, the commander here at the hospital says he'll provide me a car and maybe even a driver."

"Well, that's good. It's the right thing to see those families."

The two remained still for another few minutes before Jay began to spill his guts. "When we first landed in North Africa, we were confident. Too confident. So when we ran into the Germans in our first real big fight, we couldn't believe how good they were and how ill-prepared, raw, and undisciplined we were. Neither us GIs nor the brass had any real idea about the pace and violence of war. Almost at the start, our company commander led us into a charge across some open ground — a frontal attack — only to find the German Panzers hull down, waiting for us. They tore us apart, exploiting every advantage, every bit of cover and concealment available to them. Had one tank shot out from under me. Our soldiers were brave enough individually, but we didn't know how to really function as teams and units, or how to cover for each other as we maneuvered."

Ben could only nod his head as he remembered his first battle.

"I think I wrote you in a letter around Christmas telling you that despite all our problems, we could begin to say to ourselves, 'Enough is enough.' By that time, a lot of our original officers had been killed or wounded or relieved. The ones that took their place seemed to have a reenergized spirit, a better feel for what it would take to win. We began to understand that we hadn't come all this way to lose. I don't know where it came from or how it all happened, but with time, they got a better handle on how to fight. While most of our commanders came and went, the one who stayed with us for the duration was our one-star, Paul Robinett."

"I think you mentioned him in one of your letters."

"Yeah, I did. For most of the time we were in combat, he was the Commander of Combat Command B, 1st Armored. He was with us at all the big battles: Dejebel. Hamra, at Kasserine Pass where it was nip and tuck against Rommel himself for a while, and during the final push to capture Tunis and Bizerte where the Germans finally gave up. It was a brawl. Lot of men on both sides died. The general didn't win many friends with his bluntness, but as you can imagine, we loved him. He took a lot of heat for his tactics but the proof is we took the objectives. I think he's at Walter Reed Hospital now as he got hit about the same time I did."

"Sounds like you think a lot of him."

"Yes, I do. I'll miss seeing him and many others." Jay remained still for several minutes as he flushed out some of the demons in his soul.

"In the seven months I was there, I had five tanks shot out from under me. Had several of my men get burned up. Brodie and Jones before Christmas and then a new guy, Batten, in February. Each of them burned almost beyond recognition. Just couldn't get to those guys fast enough. Prayed they would die quickly, but from the screams we heard, well... I wrote their folks letters, but I'm still struggling with what I'll tell them when I meet them face-to-face."

"I understand. I know they'll appreciate you spending time with them. Your Silver Star and the battlefield commission connected with the deaths of these men?"

Jay looked out the window at the western Pennsylvania mountains in the distance. "Somewhat. You know how it is. Things happen quickly. We fought to the top of a hill and the Germans wanted it back. They pushed us back and then we took it back from 'em. The second time we held it for good. As you know, you do what you have to do. Truth be known, many other guys should be wearing the same medals I've got. Lot of brave men lost their lives."

Before the two men could utter another word, they heard Margaret's footsteps. "I know you two could keep talking a lot longer, but I decided I needed some information. So Jay, in one of your letters you mentioned you had been writing to Jesse Robinson. As I recall, she's a sharp young lady and I want to know what is going on there."

Jay smiled. "All in good time, my dear Mother. Did I tell you I'm learning how to play golf? They got a small course out back. Good for my therapy, my doc says. Great place to walk and enjoy the fresh air. Why don't I show you how good I'm getting while we walk over to the golf course. I'll tell you about Jesse on the way there. I promise."

"All right. We'll do that, but you promise me you won't leave out one detail about Jesse. Oh, and one more question, I didn't realize how big this hospital is until I sat outside. How many beds do they have here? Four or five hundred?"

Jay stared for a moment around the bay and at the other soldiers that shared the space with him, most of them clad in GI pajamas from which various bandages and slings, and casts protruded. "Mom, Deshon has almost eighteen hundred beds and they're all filled with heroes like the ones you see in this room. I'm one of the lucky ones. I have two arms and two legs."

Sunday, 4 July 1943
Camp O'Donnell, on the island of Luzon, Philippines

"Jim, how you doing?"

"I'm OK, Ken," Van Ostenburg said as he tried to recover from the day's struggle of moving a pile of rocks from one location to another. "Pretty much the same every day. Sweat. Move rocks. Eat a little rice and maybe a banana. Sweat. Work. Get bored. Try to sleep as I swat at some of these big black flies. Then do it all over again the next day. How about you?"

"About the same. Trying to spend more time with our senior leaders. They need encouragement like everybody else."

"What do you mean?"

"General Wainwright and the others would like to do more for the men, but the Japanese are, how should I say this, uncooperative at best. Getting really frustrated."

The chaplain grabbed a few pebbles in his hand and tossed them away, one by one. "Somehow, our guys found out by happenstance that the Japs have been receiving some Red Cross packages intended for us, but they've been stockpiling some of those supplies and breaking open the rest, then consuming the goods meant for us. When the general heard that, he went ballistic, but it didn't do him or us any good. The Jap CO just ignored his protest. Threw him out of his office. The bottom line is that if any formal agreement was signed by the Japanese government before the war about treatment of prisoners of war, it means nothing to them."

"Guess we all figured that. At least our leaders are trying."

The two men remained quiet for a time before Van Ostenburg noticed a man walking toward the senior officer's area. "You know, Ken, we've got some great leaders around here."

Chaplain Thomas smiled a bit. "You're right on that count. Take that one guy who just passed by. Johnson's his name. One of my favorites in this place, along with you and a few others. He's always upbeat no matter how bad it gets. Japs beat him up whenever they get the chance. But the man just keeps coming back. I know he's hurting like the rest of us, but to me, he is one of the heroes of this hell-hole."

"What's his background?"

"Career officer. Tough man in a quiet sorta way. Loyal to the core to his men. Lucky to have him with us. After we win this war and if he survives, he'd be the kind of man I'd like to see rising through the ranks. Got the right values."

Thomas stood up and looked at the other POWs around them. "You know my wife always wanted me to lose a few pounds, but when I look at all these fellows around here, nothing but skin and bones, so undernourished we can count almost every bone on our bodies, I don't think she had this in mind. Least, I hope not. Sometimes I don't want to look too closely at the others because I know that's what I look like too. Just skin and bones. And sores all over. And teeth falling out. Quite a mess."

The man stopped for a moment with his head down. After taking a deep breath, he stood up with some renewed energy. "See you around, Jim. Oh, I think today is July 4th. If you find out where the big picnic and the fireworks will be, you let me know."

Sunday, 4 July 1943
Chabau Army Air Corps Base, Chabau, India

"What does your crew think of the new bird?" Paul asked.

"Well for starters, that C-46 'Commando' is a big son-of-a-gun," said Keller. "No doubt about that. From the looks of it, it seems to be everything as advertised. Flies higher, farther and carries twice the load of our C-47 'Skytrains.' But the downsides are it's a lot more technical to fly and to maintain. Will take some time to figure it all out. You had a good look at it yet?"

"Not really. I'm comfortable in *The Busy Bee,* so from what you said, I'm hoping I can keep flying it until I got my missions. Trying to fly a new airplane over the mountains we got here is not something I'm looking forward to. Rather just stay where I am. Like I said, I got twenty-four missions in the C-47, so changing to a new model wouldn't be my first choice. However, if the Air Corps sends those big birds here, and if flying one of them gets me home quicker, then maybe it's a good thing. Do your pilots like it?"

"Yeah. So far. Still giving us some problems on take-offs and landings since the 46 is twice as heavy as the 47. We've been making a lot of touch-and-goes so I think we'll be all right. Not sure why they picked my crew as the one to test drive this beast, but at least we've got a headstart on everybody else if they ship 'em out here in any numbers."

Keller's tone changed. "You hear we lost two planes in the last twenty-four hours?"

"Yeah. Both on the Oboe route as they were coming back here. Didn't know either of the crews that well. Weather reports had predicted high winds with the possibility of icing. Got to be extra careful when you get that kind of warning. Could happen to any of us."

"You're right there. Least the bad weather may be keeping the Jap fighters away. They haven't made any strafing or bombing attacks in a while. Guess we can be thankful for that."

Paul glanced at some other planes spread out along the runway. "Good to see those B-24s getting stripped down so they can help us get some supplies to our Chinese friends. I'm sure those crews would rather be doing bombing missions but I'm glad we got those guys helping us."

Keller studied at a taxiing C-47 as it headed toward the end of the runway to begin its turn to takeoff. "Guess they're gonna reinforce us since I heard the other day that the higher-ups are still unhappy with the amount of supplies we're getting over the mountains. I appreciate the goals that have been set, but I'm not sure anyone up the line understands the challenges we got here: poor runways, piss-poor living conditions, and abominable weather that can bite you in the butt at any time."

He spit a big wad of tobacco on the ground before he went on. "Gotta say I appreciate General 'Hap' Arnold, the Commander of the entire Army Air Force, taking a flight over the Hump to see what we have to face every time we go up. Least he's not asking us to do something he wasn't willing to do himself."

Paul watched the C-47 make its take-off and start to gain altitude in the clear blue sky. "Yeah. Good point. My dad told me once, 'Don't ever ask a man to do something you're not willing to do yourself.' Like you said, that shows good leadership on the general's part. Anyway, gotta go. Got more work to do on my airplane. See you around, Dave. What's for chow anyway? Steak and lobster or is it dog and monkey today?"

"I'll just pretend that whatever it is, its barbeque hog and go from there. After all, it is Fourth of July. Supposed to be a good day for a picnic."

Well before dawn, Sunday morning, 4 July 1943
Fort Meade, Maryland

"Private Van Ostenburg, get up."

Without thinking, Tim tumbled out of his rack, throwing the blankets aside as he came out of his bunk to stand at attention. The platoon bay was still dark save for the one light bulb shining in each corner, the snoring of the other twenty men on the bottom floor of the two-story building still sleeping as indicated by their cacophony of nasal sounds. The clock on the wall showed it was not quite 0400.

"Van Ostenburg."

"Yes, Sergeant Ward."

"Van Ostenburg, you're a Michigan man. That makes you a damn Yankee, and you talk with an accent. Nevertheless, I'm thinking you'll fit in OK with all these men from the Commonwealth of Virginia. Lord knows that with all the crap going on in Europe, we need every good man we can find to fight Hitler, and so it's your good fortune to be selected to be in my platoon."

"Thank you, Sergeant."

"Don't thank me yet. You've been here only a week and already I like your style. Your shooting's pretty good, and now that you're part of the 175th Infantry Regiment of the 29th Infantry Division, I'm gonna treat you like all the rest of the men in my platoon. Just like dog snot. That OK with you?"

"Yes, Sergeant."

"Good. Glad you see it that way. Now since the mess sergeants are working hard to put together a good Fourth of July meal for us, they need more help. You got five minutes to get to the mess hall and report to Sergeant Crowley."

"Yes, Sergeant."

"I'm sure he's got pots and pans that need cleaning or a grease pit that needs some work or some potatoes that require peeling. That'll keep you busy and out of trouble on this day our Congress decreed a few years ago as a national holiday. Consider it my way of saying *Happy Fourth of July* to a Yankee."

As Ward turned to leave, he looked back at Tim. "Like I said, Private, I'm gonna treat you like every other man here, but since you're the new guy and you're a Yankee to boot, and we're stationed at a fort named for a Yankee general, you're gonna be gettin' some crap details until the next Yankee replacement shows up. Seems only fair. Just wanted you to know where I'm coming from."

****

At the end of the long sixteen-hour day, Tim sat on his bunk, too tired to move. His hands were raw and the grease and grime under his fingernails just didn't seem to want to come off. True to his word, the mess sergeant worked his butt off. And like Sergeant Ward said, Sergeant Crowley's grease pit was in severe need of cleaning, which required his time and energy and all the talents the young soldier could muster. That was followed by four hours of peeling spuds, one at a time. But with four other soldiers involved in that same task, all sitting under a spreading maple tree behind the mess hall, it was a good opportunity to talk to others, all dedicated to bringing this war to an end as soon as possible. Then after the evening meal was finished, the pots and pans required a good scrubbing.

Before sliding under the wool blanket on his cot, Timothy dashed off a quick note to his mother. In part it read... *Even though I've helped at home with kitchen chores for a long time, today I gained a new appreciation for the daily grind you go through to get our meals on the table every day. Thank you. I'll never take meal preparation or the serving of the meal or the clean-up afterward for granted ever again. You're the best. Thanks. Mom.*

Love you, Timothy

Even as his head hit the small pillow on his bunk, the young soldier looked forward to the next day's training as the platoon's schedule showed they would spend the day on the range, getting familiarized with the Thompson submachine gun. Because he was good with his M1 Garand rifle despite the bruised finger from one of the common missteps he made in learning about the weapon and the bolt-lock, he looked forward to seeing what the Thompson could really do. He had seen enough gangster movies to know that firing the iconic submachine gun would be a thrill. Despite his excitement, he needed some shut-eye. 0500 was four hours away.

Early Monday morning, 5 July 1943
Camp Atterbury, Edinburgh, Indiana

Mike always looked forward to the early first formation of each day. It was cooler. The sun was still below the horizon. And there was excitement in the air. While others did not relish the dawn as he did, that was their problem, not his. And now after going through basic training at Camp Atterbury, the post oddly named for a railroad mogul rather than for some long-dead general, he was one of those soldiers ordered to remain at Atterbury to be one of the first members of the newly reactivated 30th Infantry Division, a battle-tested unit from the Great War whose flag had been folded after that conflict.

As Van Ostenburg stood ready for the formation to be called to attention on his company's street, his view of the countryside was blocked by row upon row of recently assembled two-story wooden buildings, all part of the massive construction project that came on the heels of Pearl Harbor to meet the country's need to build-up its military. For Mike, it was exciting to be part of a growing Army. A minute later, his first sergeant's call for attention sounded out loud and clear.

After insuring that all his men were present or accounted for, the first sergeant announced, "Gentlemen, this morning before we begin PT, for those of you who might be interested in leaving the 30th Infantry Division and joining a different type of infantry unit, pay attention to Sergeant First Class Wright. He's a member of different kind of division. I'll let him explain. Sergeant Wright."

The strapping NCO moved quickly in front of the formation, looking at the one hundred and twenty men in the formation through piercing blue eyes, his face rugged, the outline of his jaw strong. "I am part of the 10th Light Division (Alpine). The division is unique, because as our name implies, we are a one-of-a-kind unit: Mountain Infantry. And because of the nature of the physical challenges we face in that unforgiving environment, we need a few more men to fill out our infantry battalions. If you think you have what it takes and you are interested, *and* if you can keep up with me on your PT run this morning, see me afterward. That is all."

****

After wiping the sweat from his face, Mike stood in the short line of those who wished to speak to Sergeant Wright. When it was his turn to stand in front of the man, Wright asked, "You a runner? Got to be, 'cause they're ain't many in this Army who can beat me in a five-mile

101

run and you smoked me real good today. Could be I'm getting old or maybe out of shape. What do you think, Private?"

Van Ostenburg grinned. "I don't know about that, Sergeant. All I can tell you is that I ran track in high school. High jumper also. If I volunteer for this mountain infantry you're talking about, I got a few questions."

"Go ahead. Fire away."

"Where's the training? And if I join up, will it still get me to the war?"

Wright appraised the soldier once more, the two of them about the same height, although the sergeant carried another ten or fifteen pounds of solid muscle. "Our base is at Camp Hale in the Rocky Mountains in Colorado, west of Denver. Elevation ninety-six hundred feet above sea level, though we ain't there much. Most of our training is on the rocks and snow all around Colorado. We're also scheduled at some future date to do some additional mountaineer training in West Virginia, but like I said, that's a long way off. Regarding your question about getting you to war, that decision is well above my pay grade. Can't give you a truthful answer about that except to say, that's what we all signed up for—to get to the war. Now tell me something. You a city boy or a country boy?"

"Guess I'm more of a city boy from Michigan but I know what snow and ice are all about. Done a lot of cross-country skiing. Haven't done any mountaineering or much down-hill skiing. So is it still OK if I volunteer?"

"Yeah, we'll still take you. Just sign these papers and get your gear packed. All those who sign up today will be getting on a train heading to Colorado with me in three days. You've made a good decision. We'll make a man outta you in those mountains."

Sergeant Wright grinned. "By the way, you're probably wondering why I was asking if you were a city boy or a country boy. Reason is that we let you city boys take care of our mules for a while so you can get used to those ornery creatures."

"Mules?"

"That's right. Mules. They haul a lot of our gear up and down the mountains. They're better than horses but a lot more stubborn. After you get kicked a few times you'll learn how to handle them. Now go get your gear packed."

Tuesday Evening, 6 July 1943
The Van Ostenburg home, Grand Rapids, Michigan

"Sorry, I'm late. It was a long meeting."

"That's all right. I needed a quiet day. I'm still recovering from all the emotions of seeing Jay," Margaret said. "After all these months, with all the worry about him and Jim, and now the others, I'm emotionally exhausted."

Ben put his arms around his wife. "I know. I know."

After a few moments when neither said a word, Ben slowly released her. "It's almost easier for those who go fight the war than it is for those who are left behind. Soldiers know what they are facing and have been trained to meet it head-on."

He turned to gaze out the front window as a car slowly went by. "Soldiers don't have the unknowns about what is happening to them that those who stay behind do. It is only when soldiers have a lull in the action, do they have time to worry about those back home. Hard to explain, but I hope that makes some sense."

Margaret nodded. "It does. When you were gone, I tried my best to not trouble you with all the little things going on with me or with Jim. He was such a baby then. I didn't want you to worry about us so I didn't write much about the struggles we were going through. I wanted to be uplifting and encouraging to you."

"And you did a good job with that."

"I tried. I can see the same in the letters we receive from the boys. They don't write too much about the horrors of war. Instead, they, too, try and protect us from the specifics of what they're dealing with, and I appreciate that. That's one of the reasons I wanted to give you and Jay some time alone at the hospital. I think he needed that. You two have a bond that I can't relate to. You have both experienced war. You know what it's like."

Ben walked over to look out the front window. The last streaks of dusk played with heavier clouds as deep rumbles of thunder that sounded a bit like artillery booms could be heard in the distance, preparing them for another summer storm coming their way.

"As I explained to the boys, Civil War soldiers who were in battle coined a phrase in their day. They called it 'seeing the elephant.' Combat veterans of that day and time formed an instant bond when they met another man, didn't matter if he was a Yankee or a Rebel, who had seen the elephant. Like those veterans of old, those of my generation who have seen the elephant can communicate without saying too much. We can understand each other with few words being spoken."

He turned to her. "What I'm saying is that when our sons come home in the next year or so, they'll have much inside them that will be difficult for them to get out, to speak about. They'll talk in broad generalities even when pressed to speak more about what they saw and did. Just like in the letters they send us, they will shelter us from many of the details. But when they meet other men who have seen the elephant, the two of them will enjoy a deep, almost instant, unashamed love and friendship that few could ever understand."

Ben walked back over to his wife, hugging her tightly once again. "Thank you for giving Jay and me time to share what was inside us. It is always good to let some of those long-held emotions out. A man who has gone through war needs that. You gave us a great gift. Thank you for understanding."

When they finally released each other, Margaret asked again, "So why so late tonight? Wasn't this a normal draft board meeting to look at numbers and statistics like you always do?"

Her husband retreated to his favorite chair sitting still for several moments. "It's difficult sometimes for families like ours who try to give back to this country to understand what goes through the minds of those who don't have the same kind of passion we feel. Our sons are second generation soldiers, and I anticipate their sons will follow in their footsteps if and when the time comes."

Ben stared out the front window, concentrating on the Blue stars. "You asked why I was late. Our meeting became rather heated tonight once we learned that the son of one of our more senior city officials is trying to avoid being drafted; and for some inexplicable reason, his father, this revered official, is trying to protect him. Makes me so mad I could spit!"

"So what alternatives does the draft board have?"

"Fortunately, this isn't something we see often. Fact is, nationwide the number of draft dodgers is pretty low, around four percent. But that's still too high in my book. The answer to your question is we have several alternatives. The simplest and best answer is for the young man in question to stop hiding behind his father's coattails and acknowledge he's been drafted and report as ordered."

"And if he doesn't do that?"

"We can, through legal means, make sure he serves his country in a non-combat role or have him work in a civilian work camp."

"Is there anything else you could do?"

"In the most egregious cases, we could send his ass to prison. I, for one, wouldn't mind seeing that. Too bad, we can't send the father with him."

****

Later that night, after Margaret had gone to bed, Ben sat in his favorite chair replaying Mr. Van Dyke's words. "...it's now been confirmed by multiple sources, the accounts of atrocities on the part of Japanese soldiers on British, Australian, American, and other Allied soldiers, sailors, Marines, and airmen is widespread. It goes far beyond the scope of what we first thought. In short, the Japanese have no regard for the rules of the Geneva Convention. We'll probably not know the depth of their atrocities against our men until the war's over. I'm sorry, Ben. I wish I could give you some words of encouragement, but I wanted you to hear the truth as we know it."

The old soldier remained still for most of the night, wondering how he would pass this news on to the mother of their children.

Chapter Seven

"Were so gallantly streaming"

World and National Events between
6 July and 24 December 1943

THE NOOSE AROUND GERMANY'S NECK CONTINUES TO DRAW TIGHTER
as the Allies step up their strategic-bombing campaign while ground
troops force their way onto the beaches at Sicily in Operation HUSKY
and then onto the Italian mainland in Operation AVALANCHE. On
the eastern front, Russian and German forces collide at the Battle of
Kursk, the largest tank battle in history. In late November, General Eisenhower is named the Supreme Commander of the Allied Expedi-
tionary Forces for the European theater. In the Pacific, United States
forces take major steps in the island hopping campaign with victories
at New Guinea and Bougainville.

On the home front, 530,000 coal miners go on strike, forcing the
Federal government to take over the operation of running the coalmines.

Saturday, 25 December 1943
Camp O'Donnell, on the island of Luzon, Philippines

"Any good rumors today, Jim?"

"Not a one, Ken. Maybe the Japs know it's Christmas, 'cause they seem to be cutting us some slack today. Or maybe they're tired of beating up on us. You got a read on that?"

"No. Not really. If they think they're giving us a break today, the food isn't any better than yesterday and the infirmary isn't any better than when we first got here. Got to tell you, after all this time with 'em, I still don't understand their culture or how they think. So foreign to our way of thinking."

"What do you mean?"

"I know God created all of us, both Americans and Japanese, for a purpose. But from my perspective, I'm having a hard time trying to find God's plan in all this. Guess it all goes back to trust. Got to trust God in the good times and in the bad as well. You got any ideas?"

"Hey, you're the chaplain, not me. And speaking of that, thanks for that service last night. Very meaningful, being Christmas Eve and all. Thought your story about how Joseph's brothers treated him was right on point. He's their brother. There's jealousy and hate. They decide to kill him but at the last minute they sell him into slavery. Reminded me that cruelty didn't start with the Japs. But without question, they've come up with some new ways to perfect ruthlessness."

"You're right there, but do you think most guys got the point of the message?"

Van Ostenburg scratched a festering sore on his arm before he answered. "You mean about forgiveness? That Joseph later forgives his brothers? Yeah, we heard it. Embracing the lesson around this place, well, that's another matter. Intellectually, we can understand it, but like I said, accepting the truth of that lesson is really tough right here. Maybe in time, after the war... after some time goes by... we'll see."

Chaplain Thomas sat quietly for a long time as the two men felt the day becoming warmer and more humid. "Yeah. Understand. Will take some time."

The two remained still for a few minutes drawing the increased attention from the black flies who were buzzing around their heads. After slapping a few of them away, Thomas broke their silence. "Jim, got a different question for you. A serious question."

"OK. Fire away. Got no place else to go."

"Was wondering, once this war is over, and we get home, you to your Betty and me to my Alice, what do you think you'd like to do? Stay in the Army? Start a business? Work for a big company? What would you like to do for the rest of your life?"

Van Ostenburg watched the clouds slowly drift eastward across the sky as he pondered the question. "Believe it or not, I've given that some thought. Aside from trying to survive, thinking about the future can help a man keep from losing his mind. So, yeah, I've thought of a few things."

He examined his bony arm for a minute before continuing his thought. "First, I want to spend time with Betty and raise some kids. We really only had a few weeks together before I got shipped out and then with the Jap attack and all, the last letter I got from her was back in February last year. What's that, twenty-two months? And I suspect she hasn't gotten one from me since about that same time. So we'll need to start over again as a couple."

"Makes sense. Alice and I've been married for almost ten years, but I understand what you're saying. But then what? What career are you thinking about?"

"Even though I've thought of a few things now and then, my mind keeps coming back to one thing I want to take a look at and it's your fault."

Thomas glanced over at his friend. "My fault? What do you mean?"

"It's really quite simple. Ever since the surrender at Bataan, I've watched you get beat up like the rest of us. Taking all the abuse the Japs can dish out. Eating the same rotten food as the rest of us. Living in this filth like everyone else. And yet, through it all, you face each day with a certain joy in your heart, some reservoir of hope that few others have. And because of that, you uplift and encourage the rest of us. So I guess what I'm saying, Chaplain Ken Thomas, is that maybe after all this nonsense is wrapped up, you've inspired me to look at becoming a minister. Maybe even becoming a chaplain like you."

"You really mean that?"

"Yeah, I do. Obviously I wouldn't do that without first talking it over with Betty, but that's what my heart is telling me right now. So if it's OK with you, for the remainder of our time here, I want you to give me some insights about being a chaplain. That is, of course, if you think I've got what it takes."

Thomas' head hung down, his eyes closed. He sat still for several long minutes before finally opening his eyes. "Jim, you've humbled me. If God is really calling you, then by all means, it would be my delight to do whatever I can to get you to that goal."

He looked around. "Goodness knows, we've got time for me to help coach you, teach you, pray with you, answer any and all questions you've got. Wow! You have blessed my day."

"Well, I've been meaning to talk with you about this for some time, so I'm glad you asked the question."

"You know, Jim, maybe years from now, we'll look back at all this crap we've been through only to realize that God had a purpose in all this. Tough to see right now. But maybe later... wow."

The chaplain stood up. "So for lesson number one, let's you and me go over and encourage the guys in the infirmary. They need all the cheering up we can give them. And maybe, since your voice is better than mine, you can lead the singing of a few Christmas carols."

As the two men slowly got to their feet, Thomas stopped. "You asked me a question a few minutes ago, and yes, I've heard one interesting bit of scuttlebutt."

"Yeah? What's that?"

"Seems a few weeks ago, the Japs put about a couple thousand of our guys on some trucks headed northwest. The word is they put our guys on a cargo ship bound for Japan. Not sure what all that means. Could be our troops are getting closer. Or it could mean the Japs need POWs to work in their homeland. We'll just have to wait and see, but it is an interesting rumor nevertheless. Anyway, time to go. Your first day of chaplain's school starts now."

Saturday, Christmas, 25 December 1943
Chabau Army Air Corps Base, Chabau, India

Dear Mom and Dad,

It is Christmas day here and since I'm not flying today, I thought I'd dash off a quick letter to you. Knowing the mail system, you probably won't get this until late January at best, but I wanted you to know I was thinking about you and the good Christmas dinner I'm sure you're eating.

Our Christmas dinner won't be quite like yours but our cooks are getting better, or maybe we're just getting used to what they fix. Either way, I haven't lost too many pounds so it can't be that bad.

Based on how our missions are going, I'm hoping to be finished with my tour here in the next five or six months. All depends on the weather, maintenance of our airplanes, stuff like that. A lot going on as we continue pushing supplies forward. Got more and bigger airplanes to fly which really helps.

I've gotten several letters from a girl I met while I was in Florida. I'm hoping things will work out for the two of us. Her name is Eleanor and I think you'll really like her. I know I do. A lot. I gave her your address, so don't be surprised if you get a letter from West Palm Beach, Florida. Maybe she'll write you one of these days. And yes, as you read between the lines, I think she's the one.

Hopefully you've heard from the other guys and that they are doing well. I

111

appreciate you telling me about Jay and I know you will be glad to have him home. Like you, I worry about Jim and hope we'll hear something soon.

Well, have a great day. I love you both. Oh, and one more thing. I've been promoted from Staff Sergeant to Tech Sergeant. Just got my new stripes last week. Monthly base pay jumped from ninety-six dollars a month to one hundred and fourteen. Not bad. Not many places to spend it here, but it feels good to have anyway.

Paul

After Paul sealed the envelope, he grabbed the cane the doctor had given him and slowly hobbled over to the mess hall, which also doubled as the unit orderly room, the mail room, the unit briefing room, and the operations section.

"Well there, Tech Sergeant, how is the leg feeling? What's the doc saying about when you can fly again?"

"Based on how it's feeling the last few days, I'm thinking I should be ready to go into the wild blue yonder again next week or the week after for sure. Thanks for asking, sir."

Captain Don Gaffney, one of the senior pilots in the unit, even though he had just had his twenty-third birthday, nodded. "We need you back as soon as you can, Paul. That crash you were in normally grounds a man for two or three months at least, so your recovery in three weeks is almost a miracle. You were lucky."

Paul stood still, reliving that day once again. The winds aloft from the thunderstorms whipped *The Busy Bee* back and forth, and then with them almost running out of gas, the pilot spotted Kunming through a hole in the clouds and down they went. But the angle they approached the runway was too fast and too steep. Way too steep.

They hit the runway hard, collapsing the right landing gear, the plane spinning out of control for thirty seconds which seemed like five minutes as they dug deep gouges in the Chinese hardpan. When the airplane finally came to rest, it was in several large pieces. Paul was the only survivor, with a badly twisted knee, several broken ribs, a broken nose, and severe lacerations on his face and torso. As he was flown back to Chabau on the next plane out of Kunming so their flight surgeon could patch him up, Paul reflected on his survival. Because the radio-operator position was behind the pilot's seat, he sat in a cramped cage of steel, open only on one side. While the doctors likened his living through the crash to a miracle, Paul could not help but thank the metal all around him, something the pilots in the cockpit did not have.

"Any news about the missing plane, Captain?"

"No. Nothing. Not surprising with the terrain up in those mountains like it is. All the flights are looking for any signs, but since it's been almost two weeks since we last heard from them, I wouldn't hold out much hope. If we could find the plane, maybe they'd have chance but you know how it is. They were a good crew."

"Yeah, they were. Friend of mine, Sergeant Dave Keller, was the radio man on that bird. Had only six missions left before he could go home."

Gaffney shook his head. "Understand. I knew the pilot pretty well, too. He grew up not far from me in Georgia. I grew up in Toccoa and he grew up in Clayton. 'Bout twenty, twenty-five miles apart as the crow flies. Never met 'till we got here."

Neither man had much else to say as more men began to crowd into the mess hall in the hopes of having the buffalo or cow meat prepared in such a way that it resembled a Christmas dinner back home. As Paul watched the other airmen come in, he realized *I'm one of the old guys now. No wonder most of them look so young. Almost all those who came here with me are gone. Some finished their missions fast. Some left for other units. And some others got swallowed up like Dave and his crew in the Himalayas, never to be seen or heard from again. That could have been me up there. Once I get to fly again, I've got to stay focused. I can make it. Just got to stay focused. Ten more missions to go.*

Saturday, Christmas Day, 25 December 1943
Truro, England

"You know I never gave it any thought until today, but these English folks sure do serve a great Christmas meal. Look at all these tables of food. What a spread. Surprises me that with how long they've been in this war, they've still got this much."

Tim looked over at his friend, Travis Lang, a tall, rangy fellow who hailed from the Roanoke area of Virginia, the two of them about the same age. "Got that right. It's not my mother's cooking, but the folks here have sure treated us well today. It's a great change from our regular chow."

"Yeah, but you got to feel for our cooks. You can only make SOS so many ways. But this food today is great: roast goose, Brussels sprouts, roasted potatoes, cranberry sauce, tiny sausages wrapped in bacon, all covered by this good gravy."

"Heard somebody say something about Christmas pudding for dessert. Don't know what it is, but I'm willing to give it a try."

Lang wolfed down some more of the goose. "Supposed to be a combination of dried fruits all mixed up with a lot of spices, you know, nutmeg, cinnamon, and maybe some ginger and cloves. Maybe almost like fruitcake. Not sure I've ever had any of that, but like you said, I'm willing to give it a try."

The two men continued to gulp down their holiday feast along with the other members of the 1st Battalion of the 175th Infantry Regiment in Truro's city hall. Their regiment had been the last of the 29th Infantry Division's regiments to arrive in the southwestern tip of Great Britain north of Falmouth in mid-October after making a swift voyage on board the former luxury liner, the *Queen Mary*, as part of Operation BOLERO, the build-up of United States forces in Great Britain. With the units now in place, intensive training began for the much-anticipated invasion of Europe. On this Christmas Day the townspeople of Truro decided to express their thanks to the 1st Battalion for being part of the force who would hit the beaches of France on their behalf at some later date.

While supporting so many Americans throughout their countryside who were proving to be disruptive at best and quite troublesome and unruly at other times, the people of this mining town knew the Americans were there to help put the Germans back in their place so they faced the inconveniences with a high degree of tolerance.

"Tim, as I look around, I've noticed there're some cute lasses serving us."

"Lasses are Scots, you moron. These girls are English. So yes, I saw them, too. Who could miss them?"

"Got me to thinking. Maybe we should make their acquaintance to help pass the time when we get a break from training. After all, they can only march us up and down these roads or head to the firing range so many times. What do you say?"

Van Ostenburg winked at his friend. "I'm with you. Right now, I'm particularly attracted to that redhead over in the far corner, the one serving those tiny sausages."

"Yeah, I saw her. But before you go making a fool of yourself, you should understand two things. First, where I come from, sausages fixed like this are called 'pigs-in-a-blanket.' And second, which is more important, if you really want to make a hit with that girl, you need to change your accent from that straight-forward Yankee talk to a smoother, slower Southern style of communicating, like the rest of us Virginia boys. Lord knows I thought the way we talk would've rubbed off on you by now, but I guess I'm wrong. Just thought you ought to know since I'm trying to help you out."

Tim laughed quietly as he continued to watch the girl who held his interest. Then he stood up. "Tell you what. You hold my seat. I'll be back in a few minutes."

When Tim swaggered back to the table five minutes later, he wore a broad grin. "First, her name is Gwyn, and yes, she'd like to make my acquaintance later. Her brother is in the Brit Army fighting in North Africa. Number two is there're called sausages, not 'pigs-in-a-blanket.' And most important, Gwyn said she could understand me just fine. Told me, I'm one of the few Americans in our group she could understand. Seems most of these folks here are having a real hard time figuring out what all you good ole' Virginia boys are saying because of your thick drawls."

Lang chuckled. "I think that's bull. Anyway, while you were gone cementing British-American relations, I talked to some other guys from Bravo Company. Rumor is we could be hitting the beaches in France sometime in the next two to three months. I heard what they said, but if I were a bettin' man, I'd say it would be closer to May or June unless all this rainy and wet weather ends sooner than that. What do you think?"

"I'm with you. The plus side of that is it gives us more time to get trained to go. The minus side is it also gives the Germans more time to give us some big surprises when we get there. Not looking forward to that."

Saturday, Christmas Day, 25 December 1943
The Van Ostenburg home. Grand Rapids, Michigan

"Mom, I've got to tell you, I've been dreaming about this for a long time. Yes, ma'am. A long time. Army mess sergeants try their best, but they've only got so much to work with. They can't come close to meat and potatoes like this."

"Now Jay, you're just saying that. Even though this isn't my normal

Christmas dinner, how could I possibly ignore your special request?" Margaret smiled, "I'm so pleased you are enjoying it. She thought to herself, *if he only knew how much I had to cut down on the sugar and flour and oil and butter because of the rationing over the last month to make this meal a reality. But to see his smile makes that sacrifice all worth it.*

The former lieutenant, who had received his honorable discharge papers only two weeks before the holidays, grinned. "Got to tell you, this has been my dream meal for almost a year: meatloaf and baked potatoes with plenty of butter, all finished off with warm pecan pie for dessert and red wine all around. I don't know how you did it with all the ration card restrictions these days, but thank you again," he said as he gave her a big hug.

"You know, maybe this should be a family tradition. As each one of my brothers comes home, Mom fixes him the meal of his choice. What do you think, Dad?"

"I think that's a great idea. In fact, let's make a toast to that."

And with that decree, Ben and Margaret, Uncle Bud, Jay and his significant other, Jesse, lifted a glass. They had expected Betty, Jim's wife to join them earlier, but she didn't make it until the last of the pecan pie was dished out.

"I'm sorry I'm late," she announced as she burst through the front door. "I had to meet a friend earlier today and the time got away from me. I apologize."

****

Jay and Ben left Uncle Bud snoring in the soft cushioned chair he favored as the two men stepped out the front door to begin their walk, the late afternoon clouds keeping the temperatures above freezing, melting most of the snow that had piled up from last week's blizzard.

117

Instead of taking the more familiar route, Ben turned in a different direction. "I've been taking this walk more lately. Little tougher on my leg but it's a pretty walk. And it's a little longer. Gives me more time to think."

"Think about what, Dad?"

"About you and your brothers mostly. And what kind of a country we'll be after all this is over. I don't have any doubts about us winning this war, though how long it'll take and at what price I don't know. Plain to see that when you look at a world map, between the Russians and Brits and us, we've got the Germans and Japanese in a noose that's drawing tighter every day."

"Yeah, I think you're right. Still a lot of tough fights ahead, but things are heading in the right direction."

"True, but take a careful look at these houses we're walking by. Every one of them is just like ours—two, three, four Blue stars in the windows, but I'm seeing more and more Gold stars these days. There'll be some deep scars in many families that will take a long time to heal."

Jay said nothing until they made a turn for home. "You're right about the scars. The families I talked to a few months ago will grieve the death of their sons for years. And there'll be many others who have experienced combat these past few years who will have some unseen wounds that could last a lifetime. Scars that will never be seen."

"That's true, son. Very true. It'll be hard for many of these men coming back to ever tell their loved ones what they saw, what they heard, and what they did."

Jay added nothing to that until they got closer to home. "Dad, there is something I've noticed since I've been home. Maybe you've seen it too."

Ben looked at Jay. "You're talking about Betty, aren't you?"

"Yes, sir. I can certainly understand her concern, her worry, and her discouragement. It's been what, almost two years without any word. Got to be really tough on her, especially with all the news now coming out about the way the Japanese treat their prisoners. Married for only a few months and now she knows nothing about her husband. And it's been difficult on you and mom, too. Least you have each other to lean on. Her parents helping her cope with all this?"

"Can't say for sure. While I've talked to them some, there is a different dynamic there since she's their only child. They're hard to read. Anyway, I'm concerned, but we can only do so much. I did hear recently that she was thinking of moving to Ann Arbor. Taking some classes at the university there. Not sure how that will work out."

Ben took a few more steps before he spoke again. "Now enough about Betty. She's a grown woman. Tell me about the plans you and Jesse are making."

"Well, I guess the best thing to say is we're getting serious now that my commitment to Uncle Sam has officially ended. And with the talks I've had with Mr. Vodermark, it looks like I'll be making some pretty good money real soon as he wants me to help manage some parts of the business for him."

"And so this means what?"

"It means a ring in the next few weeks and maybe an early summer wedding — that is if my best man is available."

"And who would that be?"

"Well, you, of course. Wouldn't have it any other way."

Ben smiled. "You name the date, son, and your mother and I will be there." And on that joyous note, the two men turned their attention toward brighter days and happier stories about Jay's brothers. There had been enough talk about war and its consequences for one day.

Saturday, Christmas, 25 December 1943
Camp Hale, Colorado

"Sergeant Wright, any idea when the rest of the division will get back? Me and the other guys would like to know which company we'll be assigned to."

"Van Ostenburg, regarding when the division will get back from Alaska, our division commander has not seen fit to keep me informed. And as to which unit you'll be assigned to, he hasn't provided me that information either. However, based on how well you, Oldfield, and Brooks have been doing, I've recommended the three of you be assigned to the 1st Battalion of the 87th Infantry."

"Why there?"

"Because, Van Ostenburg, that's my outfit and it's a good one. And since the three of you have met all standards for all the weapons we have and the basic mountaineering skills we require, I think the colonel will take my recommendation and put you men in my platoon, at least until you screw up. Then I'll kick your butts out if I need to."

Michael smiled. "Guess that's OK with me, Sergeant Wright. Can I ask something else?"

"I guess. Go ahead."

"Well, since I'm gonna be part of 1-87, how'd they do in Alaska against the Japs? We're hearing bits and pieces about what's been going on there, but it's hard to tell fact from rumor. So did the battalion see any action? How many Japs did they kill?"

The sergeant said nothing for a few moments as he inspected the sheath knife that he had been sharpening before the young private interrupted him.

"Fact is when the battalion deployed with the rest of the division to go attack the Japs at Kiska, I was pissed because I was already on my way to Camp Atterbury to recruit you and the other guys to fill our shortfalls. After hearing what happened there, I believe I got the better end of the stick."

"Why do you say that?"

"Because by the time our guys got to Kiska, the Japs had already abandoned the place, leaving nothing behind except some booby traps which some of our guys discovered the hard way. So while I've been helping get you and others squared away, skiing up and down the these mountains, freezing your ass off at minus thirty-five degrees as you dug your snow cave, putting you in snow shoes hauling around a heavy rucksack, and everything else, the rest of the division has been playing nursemaid to the Navy brass for the last four or five months who are hoping the Japs would be dumb enough to try and come back to Kiska."

"So they never saw any Japs?"

"That's right. Not a one based on what I've heard. So for the last few months, they've been doing some training to fill the time, but not as much as we've done here. And if I know Lieutenant Colonel Ross J. Wilson, our battalion commander, he's fit to be tied. Standing around, looking for something to keep the men busy ain't his style. You got any other questions?"

"Just one, Sergeant. Since it's Christmas Day, what time does the chow hall open?"

"In a couple of hours. So your job right now is to check on the mules you have grown to love. Make sure they've got their Christmas treat, of a couple of apples each, besides their normal hay and oats. They should like that. After you've fed them, you can eat."

***

Dear Mom and Dad,   1 February 1944
Since I last wrote you, we've been on maneuvers in the Colorado mountains

north of our base camp, west of Denver. Elevation is almost ten thousand feet above sea level. Temperatures at minus forty, not counting wind chill. Can be really dangerous if you don't know what you're doing. Fortunately for me, I've learned a lot about how to handle both the severe weather and the difficult terrain. Our only real question is when we'll get to the war. We feel like we are ready. We just want to get the word to load up and get going. Don't really care if we go east or west.

On a different note, some of the guys I've met here are snow and ski fanatics. And I confess, I'm becoming one of them. Some guys are already talking about opening up a ski resort or two when this war is all over. We all know that would take some big bucks, but from our way of thinking, it'd be great to make a living in such a beautiful part of the country. An untapped wilderness, as one of my friends describes it.

Well, got to go. Will write again when I have a chance. My love to you both. Please pass on my regard to my brothers. Michael

Wednesday, 15 February 1944
The Van Ostenburg home, Grand Rapids, Michigan

"That's a good letter from Michael. Seems to be doing well. Sounds really excited about being in the mountains."

Margaret passed the plate of carrots and corn she had canned from last year's Victory Garden to Ben along with several slices of fried Spam, this meal becoming one of their staples as they husbanded their resources for better meals whenever they had company over.

"Yes, I thought it was too, but I must confess, I can't understand why these sons of mine are so bent on fighting. I just wish they would leave the front lines to someone else."

Ben said nothing as he waited for his wife to continue.

"It's cost us so much already. Jay's wounds. Still no word about Jim. Paul flying over such dangerous mountains and now Timothy and Michael seem to want to go straight into the fight. I just have a hard time understanding why my boys feel like they do."

Ben sighed quietly to himself. He had given her his explanation before, but she either ignored his words or chose to dismiss them as male talk. "Like I said before, there comes a time in a man's life when he wants to know if he has earned the right to be called a man. Imagine if your sons were all fire fighters. Fully trained and ready to go fight a fire at a moment's notice. But the call never came. How do you think they'd feel about that?"

Margaret hesitated for a long time before answering. "Well, I suppose they'd wonder if all that training they had been through would be adequate. And I suppose they'd also wonder how good their equipment was. And if they themselves had what it would take to do the job they had been trained for."

She stopped for a moment to gather her thoughts. "Ben, I understand what you're saying, but these are my sons."

Ben grasped her hand in his. "Yes, these are our sons. God's gift to us. They are our legacy to this country which has blessed us. And because our sons know how much they have been blessed, they're willing to put their lives on the line for our country. They're warriors. And I am as proud as I can be of each one of them."

Margaret gently moved her husband's hand as she went over to the front window and stared at the Blue stars. "Everything you say is true about our boys. I guess that's why I have a difficult time forgiving those who dodge their responsibility, shirking their duties to serve this country. To serve like our sons."

She came back to the table and sat down. "A while back, you told me about one of our community officials who tried to protect his son from being drafted. What happened to that boy?"

"Guess I never did tell you, did I? Turns out that three of us from the draft board counseled that young man. After our discussion with him, he decided on his own to enlist in the Navy. Said he always loved being on the water so he signed up to be on a crew of a PT boat."

"Well, I hope he learned his lesson. I guess he's lucky that he took your advice so that he didn't end up behind prison walls someplace. Glad he's not my son. Where is he now?"

Ben stared at his wife for a long time before he answered her question. "He's in the Pacific near the Solomon Islands. He'll not be coming home. His boat, with all the rest of that crew, was sunk by a Japanese destroyer a few weeks ago. The young man's father just received notification two days ago that his son was missing in action. Seems after two weeks of searching, there have been no sightings of either the crew or the boat."

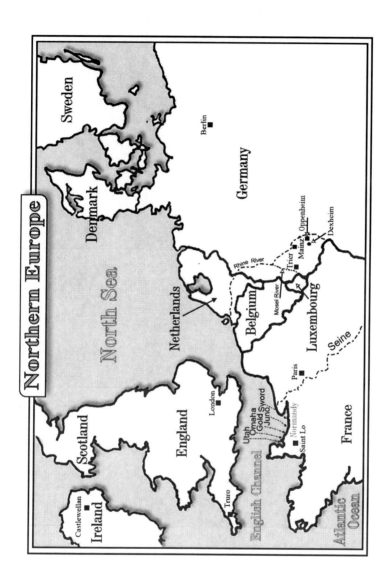

CHAPTER EIGHT

"AND THE ROCKETS' RED GLARE"

World and National Events from 16 February to 6 June 1944

WHILE THE ALLIES CONTINUE TO PRESS THEIR ENEMIES ON ALL FRONTS, the major Allied venture in this timeframe occurs on 6 June when Allied forces under the command of General Eisenhower storm the beaches on the French coast at Normandy in Operation OVERLORD.

It was also during this period that President Roosevelt signs the GI Bill of Rights providing benefits to veterans returning from the war. Additionally, the United States, Great Britain, and Australia formally protest the Japanese atrocities.

Well before dawn, Tuesday, 7 June 1944
Adrift in the Pacific Ocean east of the Ryukyu Island chain south of Japan

"Hold on, Ken... almost dawn... hang on."

"Trying to... too much oil... on my hands... and face... can't hold on much longer... too slippery... can't see."

Jim Van Ostenburg took a close look at his friend in the dim light of the stars above; his fingers now numb as he concentrated on keeping his grip tight. "I've got you by the shirt, Ken. You just keep holding onto this wood as best you can. We're gonna make it. Somehow, we're gonna make it."

Neither spoke as each tried to save his energy for what the future might bring. They had been clutching this one large piece of wood from their now demolished freighter in the oil-slicked water for almost four hours. In the last hour most of the fires on the ocean's surface around them had burned out and the cries for help from many of their fellow prisoners had gradually died away as many men gave up and surrendered themselves to the depths below.

"You still think... one of our subs... torpedoed us?"

"Probably. Either one of ours or a Brit. Who else could it have been? They had no idea that the Jap ship we were on was carrying POWs. Must have thought our boat was just carrying supplies to Japan. Can't blame the sub for blowing that tub out from under us."

"You're right... how many days... since we left the Philippines?... Three or four?"

"Three, I think. Just a guess. The way the Japs kept us crammed up in that dark hull, I couldn't tell night from day. How many guys do you figure were in that ship?"

Thomas' words came out in shorter gasps. "Heard... seven fifty... somebody said... as they marched us... to the dock."

As the first streaks of light became visible in the eastern sky, Jim heard faint sounds of someone splashing about in the water not far away. "Over here. Over here!" he hollered out.

The splashing grew closer as the survivor slowly kicked to within arm's reach. When Jim dragged the oil-covered man to their small wooden refuge, he studied his face. Within seconds, Jim was ready to push him back into the depths. It was *The Cobra*.

But before Van Ostenburg could shove his tormentor to the death he deserved, he heard the rumble of several small engines faintly in the distance. "You hear that, Ken? Somebody's out here looking for us."

Ignoring the Japanese soldier, he looked at Thomas. "Sounds like two or three small boats maybe three, four hundred yards away. Will be hard for them to spot us in these swells. They're probably Japs anyway."

"Jim... doesn't matter... start shouting... only chance... you got."

Jim's eyes narrowed as he looked at the Japanese soldier, the man too tired to offer any resistance. "What about him?"

Thomas, now losing strength rapidly, gripped Van Ostenburg's hand with all the energy he could muster before he let it go. "Jim... what's... what's your conscience... telling you?"

****

Thirty minutes later a small whale boat came alongside the two men. As Jim grasped the side of the craft, his hopes of the rescue craft being in his favor disintegrated quickly as the three Japanese sailors first hoisted *The Cobra* on board before they retrieved him and threw him on board. With the dawn now yielding more light, the two men who had been snatched from the black waters of the sea stared at each other. In that brief moment, Jim saw something in the other man's eyes he had never seen before. *What does that look mean?*

As the small boat bounced about in the choppy waters and the seamen hauled three more POWs on board, the look on *The Cobra's* face never changed as he continued to stare at Jim. It was only when the Japanese sailors seemed ready to send one of the POWs who appeared to be near death back overboard that *The Cobra* took his eyes off Jim as he barked at the sailors in his commanding Japanese tone. And to his surprise, Jim watched as the sailors reluctantly moved his fellow POW safely away from the gunnel of the small boat and renewed their search for others. When they found no more survivors, Jim thought *God, why did you save me so that this nightmare could continue? Which one of us is better off, Ken or me? How long, Oh Lord, how long will this ordeal last? What are you teaching me through all this?*

D-Day +1, Tuesday, 7 June 1944
Omaha Beach, Normandy

The men on the LCVP, the Landing Craft, Vehicle, Personnel, their average age eighteen, were quiet as they neared the beach, their attention on the sailor steering their assault craft as he tried to stay in formation with those other boats on his left and right. The men also noticed that the sailor was doing his best to maneuver around the floating corpses which became more numerous the closer they got to the beach. Even though D-Day had been twenty-four hours earlier, evidence of the invasion was everywhere.

As they got closer to the beach, Sergeant Ward waved his arms about to grab his platoon's attention before the ramp of their LCVP was about to go down. Above the noise of the boat, he shouted out, "Remember, like I told you before, when the ramp goes down, get out fast. Head directly away from the beach toward that man you see waving that blue flag in front of us. Go straight toward that guy. If you take fire, keep moving toward the blue flag. Don't stop till you get there."

When the moment arrived and the ramp fell, Van Ostenburg and his friend, Lang, bounded forward only to find themselves in chest-deep water, but they knew what Ward said. Move fast toward the man waving the blue flag. Though weighed down by over sixty pounds of equipment on their backs, and their woolen uniforms soaked, they sloshed though the shallower water, walking faster and faster until they reached dry sand. Still moving toward the blue flag, Lang was the first to notice the bodies lined up near the water's edge, giving evidence of what had taken place on Omaha Beach a day earlier.

"You see 'em, Tim? Could have been us if we'd been in the first wave."
"I know. I know," said Tim as he tried to keep his eyes forward. But despite his best efforts, like the rest of the men in his platoon, they could not ignore the reality of war all around them.

Sergeant Ward was counting his men as they trudged up from the beach, and once he had all his men accounted for, he halted the platoon a short distance from the blue flag, a spot where they could see the sandy beach and the high, steep grassy bluff looking down on them from above. Their eyes saw demolished vehicles and deep holes in the ground caused by both Allied and German artillery and mortar and naval gun fire. They could make out arms and legs torn from the bodies of unnamed soldiers half-buried in the sand near them. They spotted punctured helmets, shattered M1 rifles, red-stained bandages, canteen cups ripped to shreds, and torn, unused gas masks. They noticed bits of paper lying all around, torn and shredded letters, photographs, toilet paper, newspapers and money. Green Army blankets slashed, chocolate bars from K-rations split apart and covered with sand. Toothbrushes and combs lying about. They watched as streams of medics came down from the bluff above carrying litters back toward the beach, each filled with an American soldier.

And they smelled the mix of death and blood and cordite and smoke and gas and burning rubber and vomit and the salt air of the sea all becoming one omnipresent stench. They heard the moans of their comrades who lay in those litters as they passed by. The shouts and the orders of officers and sergeants and beach masters charged with moving men and equipment either toward the beach or away from it filled their ears from multiple directions as these leaders directed bulldozers to shove damaged pieces of equipment out of the way so more tanks and jeeps and trucks could come ashore unimpeded. And in the distance, to the south and southeast, the thud and crash of artillery rounds impacting and the clatter of machine gun fire further inland only added to the confusion and the chaos yet to come.

Tim muttered under his breath *My God, look at this! Is this what Dante's inferno looks like? How did anyone live through this?*

But then he caught sight of a ragged group of thirty or forty unarmed men sitting on the ground with their hands on top of their heads and U.S. soldiers around them. "Travis, look there. German POWs?"

Lang stared at the group. "Yeah, must be. They're no older than us. Don't look too tough right now, but considering all this around us, it must have been a horrific fight."

When Sergeant Ward sensed that his men had seen enough, he spoke in a quiet voice. "Yesterday, the 116th Regiment of our division landed here on Omaha Beach along with the 1st Infantry Division and part of a Ranger battalion. Some of the men from the 116th never made it to where we stand. Some didn't even make it to the beach. The captain told me last night that Company A, 1st Battalion of the 116th was almost totally wiped out. Some of you know those men. Many of them from around Bedford, Virginia."

Then Ward's tone changed dramatically, both in volume and intensity. "I tell you this for two reasons. First, there are no more fun and games. Training is over. The Germans mean business. But so do we. Remember what you've seen here today. Now we're gonna move up that trail to the top of the bluff and go where the company commander tells us to go. Let's show the Germans what we're made of. Stay focused. Keep your eyes open. Now follow me."

Early Sunday evening, 19 June 1944
Jacksonville, Florida

Paul and Eleanor giggled like school children as the train's engineer blew his whistle, signaling their arrival at the station in the growing city of Jacksonville, Florida. The last week had been a whirlwind for the two of them, starting with Paul's late night arrival back into Morrison Field in West Palm Beach five days earlier. After a long, hot shower, a quick change into a fresh uniform, and an expensive long-distance telephone call to his mom and dad, the Technical Sergeant rushed over to Eleanor's home and proposed. A justice of the peace cooperated with their desires and married the couple the next day, and now they were bound for Grand Rapids to meet Paul's folks.

"Paul, you did tell your folks I was coming with you, didn't you? And that we're married?"

"Yes. Of course, I did. On both counts. I know my mom's really excited about meeting you since the two of you have become such good pen pals."

"Well, I certainly hope so. Did you tell them about your knee?"

"No, not a word. A lot of guys got problems a lot worse than mine. Besides, it's not like they're gonna kick me out of the Army Air Corps. Like the doc said in India, with time and some rest, it'll get better. Within a month or so, I probably won't be limping at all. And flying is no problem. Hasn't slowed me down yet. Anyway, enough of that. Let's go grab some good old American food from the dining car, and then after that, let's adjourn to our drawing room," he said as he gave her a quick grin. "I think, Mrs. Van Ostenburg, we need to see how much exercise my knee can take."

Late Sunday afternoon, 19 June 1944
Camp Swift, Texas

Half a continent away from the train taking Paul and his new bride to Grand Rapids, another locomotive slowed down as it towed eleven passenger cars into the outskirts of Bastrop, Texas, forty miles east of Austin, the small town the home of one of the Army's newest camps.

Aptly named Camp Swift, its twenty-one hundred buildings had risen from the dusty Texas hill country in one hundred and eight days, shortly after the outbreak of the war.

As the soldiers tumbled off the train, one of them asked, "Sergeant Wright, how hot is it? Heard somebody say it was pushing one hundred and twenty degrees. And look how flat it is. Nothing here but flat ground and hundreds and hundreds of wooden barracks. How many guys they got here anyway?"

"Van Ostenburg, you never stop asking questions do you? Number one, you're a tough guy so you can handle the one hundred degree plus temperatures. And as far as how many men can be trained here, the answer is there are enough buildings, they can house almost ninety thousand soldiers at a time. And because a bunch of guys have shipped out to Europe, they got space for us. Now, if you don't mind, I've got work to do." Turning away from the young soldier, Wright ordered his men to fall into formation.

Next to Michael stood Private George Middleton, a lanky former logger who had grown up in eastern Oregon. Wiping the sweat from his face, Middleton spoke softly, "I hope this is the last stop we make before we finally get into the war. Gettin' tired of seeing so much of the United States. Joined this outfit to fight Japs or Germans and we ain't seen any of them yet. Why do you suppose they sent us here?"

Before Michael said a word, Sergeant Wright addressed his platoon. "All right, get your gear unpacked in this barracks building behind me. It's L-184. Remember that if you get lost. The chow hall down the company street will be open for another hour. Eat and then get some rest. First formation tomorrow will be at 0530. Reveille at 0500. Road march with full combat pack. Since this is our first day here and we're not used to the heat, we'll take it easy." Sergeant Wright smiled. "Only gonna do twelve miles in three hours. Fall out and get some rest."

Later, after eating a surprisingly good meal of fresh beef, vegetables, and hot rolls, Michael and his friend sat on their bunks double-checking their gear for the next day's road march. "Hard to believe all the training we've done in the last six months. First in the mountains of Colorado, then the rock climbing in West Virginia in April, back to Colorado in May in time for the spring weather, and now here in the middle of 'Nowhere' Texas in the heat of summer. Makes me wonder if the Army will ever let us fight."

"I'm with you, Mike. No question we've been putting in the miles. For me, I have to say I liked West Virginia the best. Seneca Rocks was a beautiful place. Know you must've liked those mountains, too. You were like a mountain goat climbing those steep cliffs. It true you made it up both *Black Mamba* and the *Fine Young Cannibals?* They're rated at what, 5.13?"

Van Ostenburg nodded, remembering the sheer drops on both of the climbs and the ratings systems used for mountaineering: 5.1 the easiest, going up to 5.13 the toughest. "Yeah, a couple of us did 'em both. Had some places that took my breath away, that's for sure. Like you said, West Virginia is a beautiful state, but for me, once this war is over, I'm heading back to Colorado. It's a great place to dream about, but right now we need to get this war over with first. Let's get some rack time. Dawn will be here soon."

Dusk, Monday, 20 June 1944
Approaching Kyushu Island along the
southwestern coast of Japan

Jim sensed the freighter slowing down even though he was well below deck in the cavernous hull of the stinking ship. *Wonder where we are? Have we finally gotten to the mainland? What will they do with us now?*

"What do you think, LT? We gettin' ready to dock?"

"Guess we'll know soon enough, Johnnie. Feels like it, since they put us on this tub, what, 'bout five days ago?"

Staff Sergeant Johnnie Patrick, a thin but energetic fellow, looked around at the men packed around them, hardly room for the one hundred and fifty POWs to stand. It had been that way since the Japanese plucked them out of the water after their first ship was sunk. "Can't get too much worse. We're breathing nothing but our own sweat and urine and feces and all they're feeding us is mouthful of rice and little water. I just hope we dock soon. Ready to smell a little fresh air. Got to stretch my leg some, too."

"How's the leg?"

"Seems a little better. Spending some time in the salt water after we got hit may have helped it. Swellings gone down some. Speaking of that, me and others are sorry Chaplain Thomas didn't make it. Know he was a friend of yours. A good man. Kept a lot of us from losing our senses. And he was a good storyteller, too. He had a way of keeping our minds off our circumstances, if you know what I mean."

Jim nodded, remembering the man and some of their last conversations.

"We need somebody to take his place."

"What do you mean?"

"You know, we need a new morale officer. Somebody we respect. Me and the other NCOs been talking, and we've decided you're gonna be Chaplain Thomas' replacement. Got to have somebody to help keep us all moving forward and to make some sense out of all this. So like I said, we picked you."

Van Ostenburg stared down at what was left of his feet, both of them scarred, bruised, blistered, and swollen. Like almost all those around him, what was left of his tattered uniform barely covered his skin and bones.

"Johnnie, I appreciate the confidence, but you know I'm a grunt. An

Infantryman. I'm not a chaplain. I'm not trained to do what Chaplain Thomas did."

"Yeah, we know that. But you've got a good heart and a good head on your shoulders and, most importantly, we trust you. That means more to us than any degree or title. We know you'll do what you can for us, at least as much as the Japs will let you, that is. Anyway, we had a sort of informal vote and you're it. Didn't consider anyone else."

****

"Where you figure they're taking us, LT? Been on these rickety trucks for a good four hours. Seems like we're heading north, then maybe east some. Can't tell for sure."

Like the rest of them, Jim bounced up and down as they sat in the bed of the old, dilapidated truck, theirs one of six vehicles the men had been loaded onto as soon as their freighter docked several hours after dusk. "One of our guys who understands some Japanese said he saw a sign when we first got to the trucks. Thinks it may have said Nagasaki, but he couldn't be sure. Definitely was a good-size port. Got a quick glimpse of some big Jap ships in the harbor."

"Yeah, I saw 'em. Looked like they're listing a bit to one side. Hope so anyway."

For the most part of the next two hours the men were quiet as they breathed in the clean, fresh night air, glad for what time they had to spread out a little and stretch their limbs. With the aid of the light of the stars and the moon, they could see that the countryside was a mix of hills and valleys. The air grew cooler as the trucks climbed up the not-so-wide dirt road, the old vehicles dipping in and out of numerous deep potholes. Then the small convoy staggered to a halt at a small intersection on a slight rise.

137

As soon as the trucks stopped, the Japanese guards gestured for all the POWs to get off the trucks and stand in formation facing the east where the first rays of the rising sun could be seen. *The Cobra* took command of the formation, walking back and forth in front of the prisoners, his swagger not the same as the POWs had been accustomed to, as the man now walked with a noticeable limp.

After ten minutes of silence, another man marched up in front of the formation, this one in the green dress uniform of a Japanese officer, his uniform blouse adorned with ribbons of various colors. After he and the guard exchanged salutes, the officer stared at the prisoners in front of him for several minutes, allowing them to study him just as he studied them. When the officer finally spoke, he addressed the prisoners in precise English, because, as they learned later, he had been schooled in Chicago in the early 1930s.

"My name is Major Asao Fukuhara. I am the Camp Commander of Fukuoka Prisoner of War Camp, Number Seventeen, between Nagasaki and Fukuoka. We anticipated hosting more of you, but it seems one of your own submarines killed many of your comrades. Too bad. You will be our guests here for the foreseeable future. Along with Australian, Dutch, and British prisoners who have been with us for some time, you will have the privilege of working in the Mitsui Kozan Miike Kogyo-Sho coal mine. As long as you cooperate during your stay with us, we will be most generous in providing you food, medical care, shelter, and even a small monetary compensation for your efforts. You will work twelve hour shifts mining the coal we require. My soldiers will now march you to your barracks. You will be introduced to the mine later today."

Just after dusk, Thursday, 30 June 1944
Five miles northwest of St. Lo, France

"See anything, Sarge?" the man whispered.

"No," the young sergeant said quietly as he kept his eyes moving from right to left and then back again. "But that doesn't mean they're not out there. With all that artillery and mortar fire going on east and west of us, you can bet they're awake and looking for us just like we're looking for them. They've fooled us before, so stay real quiet and use your eyes and ears."

"OK, Sarge," the eighteen-year-old private murmured. Sergeant Tim Van Ostenburg did not know much about the fellow except his last name was Gorman, he was from someplace in Ohio, and he joined the battalion only three days ago. With so many replacements coming these last three weeks, Tim had felt no need to get any more information than that. Maybe later that time would come.

"Oh, Lord, what's that?" the private asked in a voice louder than necessary.

Tim listened closely with a practiced ear. "German MG-42. Called a Spandau. Can lay down a lot of bullets real quick. Really good machine gun. Sounds like its maybe a kilometer—a thousand meters—a little over a half a mile—to the east."

"Shouldn't we report that since we're way out in front of the company? You know, listening and looking for anything important? Maybe I should go back and tell the company commander what we heard?"

Tim whispered, "No. First of all, the CO probably heard it just like we did. Second, our job is to report anything we see here, close by. Sit still and listen. Stop moving around."

As Tim searched the area around them he thought, *Where do replacements like this kid come from? Who trained them anyway? Wish Sergeant Ward was still around. And Lang. And the rest. Only four of us in our platoon left from that day we came ashore at Omaha Beach. What was that? Three, four weeks ago? Lot of good men are gone, leaving a long trail of blood and guts. And for what? We moved fifteen, twenty miles back and forth and we still haven't come close to taking St. Lo. And now we're a company filled with replacements like this kid. Got some training, but not nearly enough.*

If the brass really wants us to take St. Lo, the company needs to get pulled off line for a week so we can get these new guys squared away so they don't get themselves killed in the first thirty seconds when somebody shoots at us. Need to tell the new company CO next time I see him, unless he's gone, too, replaced by another one filled with piss and vinegar trying to make a name for himself.

For the next thirty minutes the night remained quiet except for the young soldier shifting around in his position, each time incurring Tim's wrath. "Gorman. Stay still."

"Just trying to get comfortable. And now my canteen's empty."

"We're not here to be comfortable... Tell you what. Since we're gonna be staying here all night, you take your canteen and mine and move real quiet-like back to that stream we passed near the farmhouse just over that rise to our rear. Fill up our canteens and be back in fifteen minutes. You think you can do that?"

"Yes, Sergeant."

"Good. Fifteen minutes. If you get in trouble, fire that M-1 of yours two times. If I get in trouble, I'll do the same. When you're coming back, the password between you and me is you say 'one' and I'll say 'four.' You got that? One and four."

"Yes, Sergeant."

"Good. Move out slow and easy. Fifteen minutes."

Tim turned to watch the man work his way in an acceptable manner through the vines and branches that camouflaged their observation post. It was quiet, perhaps too quiet.

****

Twenty minutes later Van Ostenburg heard a slight rustling of branches behind him from the direction he expected the private. He waited until he heard some more noise. Knowing how scared the young soldier must be, Tim whispered, "Four." With no response, he raised his rifle in the direction the sound came from. Just as he was about to give the password one more time, a new racket came from behind him. Before he could react, three soldiers dressed in the uniform of the *Wehrmacht* materialized out of the gloom and surrounded him. In passable English, one of them said with a grin, "We'll take your weapon now."

Early afternoon, Monday, 4 July 1944
The Van Ostenburg home, Grand Rapids. Michigan

Although Ben was not gifted in the art of taking photographs, he felt his old Kodak was still good enough to take pictures of the two new married couples and Margaret under the shapely maple tree. He just hoped that when they got the prints back from the processor, they would be acceptable. Even as he looked through the viewfinder he announced, "Sure am glad I'm blessed with two more beautiful daughters-in-law. You two balance out the looks of those two you married."

Margaret quickly jumped to the defense of her sons. "Now, Ben, these two handsome gentlemen look just fine. And not only that, since Jay and Paul got married, I've never seen them smile more."

"That's right, Mom. You tell him," said Jay, smiling.

And after five or six tries, the chronicle of the day in pictures was complete. With that task accomplished, everyone's attention turned to good food, good conversation, and the joy of welcoming the two wonderful young women into the Van Ostenburg family. Margaret, as only she could, guided the conversation to old stories about their husbands.

An hour before the sparklers were to be lit, Ben nodded at the two boys, signaling his desire to take his walk, and off they went.

****

After they walked the first block in silence, Paul commented, "Dad, I'm sorry I wasn't here when Uncle Bud died. The doctors figure out what happened?"

"No. Not exactly. While your uncle carried some extra weight around for a long time, I think it was most likely his dealing with the loss of your aunt. That's got to wear on a man. I'm sure if or when something like that ever happens to your mother, for me there will be an emptiness that can't be filled. And like I've told others through the years, while we think we might act or react in one way or another to a death of our spouse, I don't think any of us will really know until that happens. Too many variables."

Ben walked in silence for another half-block before he smiled. "Got to say, you two have married some wonderful women. What a blessing they are."

"Yeah, you got that right," said Jay before he added a few steps later, "Haven't seen Betty in a while. How is she doing?"

"Not sure. Haven't seen her myself in a few months. Talk to her folks now and then, but they're pretty close-lipped. She's living in Ann Arbor now, and like us, I don't believe she's heard anything from Jim. We keep hoping and praying. We've talked to others who are in the same boat as us, so we know we're not the only ones dealing with this. Haven't mentioned it to your mother, but I'm thinking we might not know anything, good or bad, until the war's over." After a few more steps, he added, "And it's possible we may never find out anything."

"It's like that with the air crews flying the Hump," Paul said. "We're pretty much resolved to the fact that if we went down in those mountains, the remains of our plane might never be found. Just get swallowed up in the vastness of the terrain. Same goes with air crews that go missing over the ocean. Their stories known only by God. Just the way it is."

As they made a turn onto another street that Paul had not been on in several years, the number of Blue and then Gold stars and pennants caught his attention. "I'm looking at these windows remembering some faces and some names. Didn't realize so many had served and so many had died."

"You're right, son. Grand Rapids has played its part, no doubt. From what I know about some of these Gold stars you see, one is for a crewman on a freighter sunk in the North Atlantic by a German sub while ferrying supplies to England. That one over to your left is for Jim Wocjikowski, a tail gunner on a B-24 whose plane was shot down on a mission over Truk Island in the Pacific two months ago. And the house next to it has a Gold star for a man who was a medic in the paratroopers, a soldier killed in the first few hours of the invasion into Sicily. None of these men had reached their twentieth birthday when they were killed."

After one more block, the three men turned around. "Paul," Jay asked, "you mentioned you're supposed to be in Chanute Air Base in a week. Where is that? What will you be doing there?"

"The base is about fifty miles or so south of Chicago and I'll be one of the instructors in the communications school there. Right now there are twenty-six skills our commo guys must know, some depending on what aircraft they'll be flying or where they'll be stationed. I suspect I'll be helping teach a number of subjects. Won't know which ones until I get there."

"You and Eleanor looking forward to it?"

"Absolutely. A new place for both of us, and of course, just to have a chance to be together is a dream come true."

With home now in sight, Paul added, "Dad, thanks for letting me read those letters from Tim and Mike. While they weren't too wordy, at least we know where they are. Got to be frustrating for Mike, but it sounds like he's in a real specialized unit. Got to admire him. Not many units can get to where they can road march twenty-five miles in eight hours with a full pack and one hundred degrees. Takes some tough guys to do that. Since the war isn't over yet, I'm sure there's a place for that unit. Got to watch out for what you wish for."

Late Monday afternoon, 15 August 1944
The Van Ostenburg home. Grand Rapids, Michigan

Ben got home later than he intended. It was a day which required all the patience he could muster as one of his customers could not understand why Ben could not order a certain part their radio required to make it work. And so rather than send the woman away in an unhappy state, he gave her a better radio at cost. And he knew the woman would be pleased that she could now listen to Kate Smith belt out Irving Berlin's *God Bless America* whenever it came on the radio.

After searching the house for Margaret with no results, he stepped out the back door and saw her sitting on their old swing, rocking slowly back and forth as she stared into space. "Are you OK?" he called out.

When she turned to him, he saw tears running down her face before he saw the telegram in her hand. He sat down next to her and gently took the flimsy piece of paper in his hands. The document was from the Red Cross. He scanned it quickly before he read it a second time, word for word.

"...your son, Sergeant Timothy Van Ostenburg, Service number 374560836, is now a prisoner of war and is being held by German Army forces. As we receive information regarding his whereabouts, we will provide that to you..."

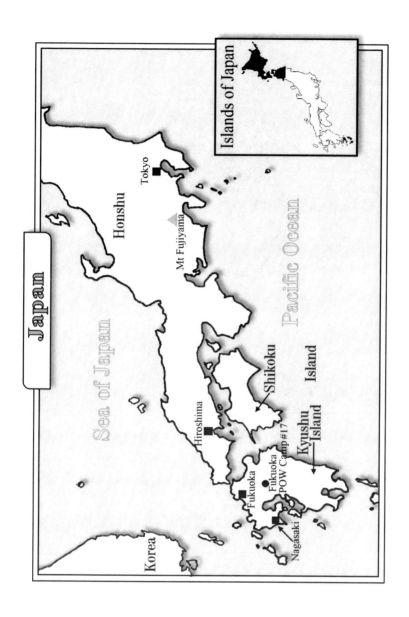

Islands of Japan

Japan

Honshu

Tokyo

Mt Fujiyama

Sea of Japan

Pacific Ocean

Shikoku
Island

Hiroshima

Kyushu
Island

Fukuoka
POW Camp #17

Fukuoka

Nagasaki

Korea

Chapter Nine

"The bombs bursting in air"

World and National Events between
16 August and 15 December, 1944

ALLIED FORCES LIBERATE PARIS AND BRUSSELS IN THE FALL OF 1944 while an Allied offensive to gain a significant port, Operation MAR-KET GARDEN, suffers major casualties. Massed Soviet forces drive through Eastern Europe toward Berlin, causing heavy losses to the German Army. Unbeknownst to the Allied commanders, during this period the Germans prepare a major offensive known as the Battle of the Bulge against U.S. and British forces in Western Europe. In the Pacific theater, the United States island hopping campaign continues with landings at Peleliu and in the Philippines. U.S. Naval forces deal a critical blow to the Japanese Navy at the Battle of Leyte Gulf, while B-29 bombers strike the Japanese mainland from bases in China.

Late afternoon, Friday, 16 December 1944
German Kaserne, east of Trier, Germany, along the Mosel River

"They give you any food before they threw you in here with us?"

"Small cup of some broth. Better than I expected. 'Course I've been

147

E and Eing for the last day and a half; you know trying to escape and evade, but they caught me early last night."

"Judging by your flight suit, you've got to be a pilot. What airplane?"

"P-47. Was on escort mission with some B-17s headin' for Berlin when I got shot down."

Sergeant Tim Van Ostenburg and his companion, Corporal John Townsend, a native of Kansas City, Kansas, a paratrooper from the 82nd Airborne Division, studied their new guest. The man was not quite as tall as them, but certainly more well-nourished, wore an aviator flight jacket singed on one side from some burn marks. "Glad you got down OK. Regarding the food, get used to it. Pretty much our daily meal with some crusty bread and some cheese every now and then two times a day. And if we're lucky, maybe some sausages every other day or so. They're pretty good."

The newcomer nodded as he surveyed the cell he found himself in along with the other two men. The space was twelve feet by twelve feet. One window with heavy metal bars let in what daylight there was along with the cold air. In one corner was a small hole in the floor. Judging by the noxious odor coming from it, the new man correctly identified it as the community crapper. He also noted that, like himself, each of his fellow cellmates had been given only one holey woolen blanket to ward off the cold.

The pilot held out his hand. "Name's Joe Richardson. 56th Fighter Group."

Tim and his companion stared at Richardson for a moment. "Lieutenant, we hope you don't take this the wrong way, but two weeks ago the Germans tried to pull one over on us. Planted a stoolie in here with us; trying to pump us for some information. We figured it out pretty quick and so, if you don't mind, we need to have a little discussion with you before we get too chummy. Like I said, we mean no disrespect, but... where'd you come from back in the States?"

****

After an hour of grilling Lieutenant Richardson, Tim shook the pilot's hand. "Lieutenant, we appreciate you being patient with us, but you can understand our concerns. Seems like the Germans have almost forgotten us. Since you're a pilot and being an officer and all, we figure they'll be shipping you out pretty quick, so before they do that, what can you tell us? Over the last several weeks, the Germans seem to be moving a lot of men and equipment west toward France, which doesn't make a lot of sense to us. So what can you tell us 'bout that? And how's the war going anyway? Our guards are smiling a lot lately, so we're not sure what to make of that. For us, it's been pretty boring, since like I said, it seems as though they've forgotten about us."

"How long you guys been POWs anyway?"

"About six months. Caught us in late June. Our first stop after getting captured was outside Paris. Then in the middle of the night, they stuck us on a truck and dumped us off at some prison somewhere near the French-Luxembourg border before they brought us here. Been here since early November. So here we sit, trying to keep each other sane and learning some German from the guards. Figure they'll move us into Germany sometime, but who knows when."

"Well, let's see what I can tell. First, my name is Joe, so let's keep it that way. None of this lieutenant stuff." Richardson smiled, "And as you know from your questions, I'm from Charleston, South Carolina. Know I'll have to listen real close to what you two are saying since both of y'all have funny accents."

Townsend laughed, "Yeah, we've noticed you talk funny yourself. But like Tim asked, what's going on? Are we winning the war? Any idea how much longer this will go on? We keep looking for a chance to escape, but nothing's come our way so far."

Richardson glanced once more at the concrete walls and the one window, "Well, I can see how getting outta here could be tough. Anyway, overall, we're kicking their butt."

The pilot looked at his two companions for a moment. "I don't have to tell you two about Normandy. You were there and I wasn't. But since our guys broke out of that peninsula around August, for the last few months we've been pushing the Krauts further and further back toward their homeland. Not sure why the guards here would be optimistic about anything so I can't speak to that. The war's not over yet, but there's a lot of scuttlebutt that says once we push the Krauts back across the Rhine, they'll surrender. Since I'm just a dumb fighter jock now stuck with you guys, guess we'll just wait and see."

Tim stood up and looked at their cell window. "What about the war against the Japs? What's going on there?"

"Can't answer too many specifics about that except it's my understanding our guys are moving from one island to another, getting closer with each one to the Japanese mainland. Calling it 'island hopping.' Heard our heavy bombers are now hitting the Japs everyday just like we're doing to the Germans."

"What about the Philippines? One of my brothers was there when the Japs invaded in late '41. Unless something's changed since I last got a letter from my folks, there's been no word about him."

Richardson gave a slow nod, but said nothing for several minutes, his eyes staring hard at the floor. "Been some big battles on those islands. MacArthur's men landed in Leyte in October so that's good. Your brother at Bataan or Corregidor?"

"Bataan, I think."

"My oldest brother three years older than me, a Citadel graduate, was on Corregidor. An Army Captain. Like your family, we haven't heard anything about him since March '42. Nothing at all."

Saturday evening, 24 December 1944
Fukuoka POW Camp, Number Seventeen,
Island of Kyushu, Japan

"LT, my ears are still ringing from all that noise inside the mine, but they're still good enough to hear those bombers flying overhead. Can't tell what kind they are since they're so high up. What do you figure? B-24s or something else? They've got to be, what, twenty thousand feet up there at least?"

"Not sure about the plane, but I'm thinking you're right, Johnnie. Got to be twenty thousand feet plus. Since they're coming from the west, maybe our guys are using China as a base. One thing is certain. These Jap guards are spending a lot more time looking up instead of seeing how we're doing."

"You think they might move us again some time?"

"Could be, but I don't see it that way. They need every bit of coal we can pull out of their mine. We're too valuable to 'em right where we are. Jim stared out into space as he pondered that thought. *Here we sit. Eighteen hundred guys boxed in here real tight. Two hundred yards by maybe a thousand. Getting fed a cup of rice, some radish soup and a few potatoes thrown in every now and then. Least we all got a place to sleep even if it is fifty or sixty guys in each building. Tar paper roofs. And they work us twelve hours a day no matter what. And they give us five cigarettes each day.*

"But you know the bright side of all this, Johnnie?"

"No, sir. What's that?"

"This is a great improvement over Camp O'Donnell."

"Yeah, hadn't thought about that. See, that's why we made you the morale officer. I feel better about this place already. Speaking of the differences between the Philippines and here, I heard the Jap doc here is using some of our guys who were medics to help him out. That true?"

"Yep. Sure is. That Aussie, Major Smythe, went to bat for us with the

151

camp commander. Told him that maybe the Japs might get more production out of us if we had better medical care and that we had some guys who could help. So, despite how tough Major Fukuhara can be at times, he bought into that logic. Has definitely helped out a few of our guys who were in bad shape. Not all of 'em, but at least some."

"I know the men appreciate it."

"Then tell our guys to thank Major Smythe. He's the one who pushed it through. And truth be known, I think it was him who pushed the Japs to hand over some of those Red Cross packages that have been sent for us. He's a good man. Loyal to the core on anything that'll help us out. Right now, he's trying to get us some blankets before winter sets in. Even saw him face down one of the guards the other day as the guy was kicking one of his Aussies around while we were in the mine."

"Wow. Hadn't heard that. Speaking of guards, I haven't seen *The Cobra* around too much. Where's he been?"

"No idea. Just know I don't miss him."

"Heard a story the other day. Is it true you hauled him out of the ocean when we got torpedoed on the way here?"

Van Ostenburg stared at the moon as it began to make its presence known over the hills around them, remembering Ken Thomas losing his battle to hold on as the oil-slicked swells of the ocean sapped all his strength from him that morning; remembering the sounds of *The Cobra* struggling in the water trying to survive and of Jim's battle within his conscience.

"Yeah, I did. Seemed like the right thing to do at the time."

Mid-afternoon, Saturday, 24 December 1944
German Kaserne, east of Trier, Germany along the Mosel River

"Man-oh-man. From what I can tell, the Brit bombers are tearing the town apart. How long is this gonna last?" John Townsend shouted above the noise of the low-level passes of the British Lancaster bombers and the accompanying P-47 fighters as they zoomed overhead before making another bombing run at the road junctions and railroad complex near the center of Trier.

Joe Richardson looked out through their window, trying to identify the units that were doing the bombing. "Kind of surprises me that they're dropping bombs here again after the big strike they made four, five days ago? Must be something about this area they're going after."

"You think maybe that with the offensive the Germans just launched, we're sitting on one of their main supply lines?"

"I was thinking the same thing, Tim. Matter of fact, during a couple of our mission briefs before I got shot down, our fighter group intel officer was making a big deal about the major roads leading in and out of Germany. Now that I think about it, Trier was one of those places he talked about."

The three watched as another P-47 flew by so close that they could almost see the pilot grin as he blazed away at his target. "You know, the more I think about it, this attack makes sense. The flattest ground for both the rail lines and the roads is in the valley of the Mosel as it winds its way from the Rhine toward France and Luxembourg. That would explain why our guys are trying to choke up the rail lines and the roads running through here."

Thompson asked, "So what do you mean, Joe?"

"What it means is that our boys are trying to stop German supplies from moving in either direction and they can do it by blowing up all the roads and rail lines right here. I just hope they concentrate their firepower on their targets in town and stay away from our little kaserne. If they put their bombs where they're supposed to, we'll be OK. But if they miss and land a few near us, it wouldn't take much to blow some of these old stone walls down, crumbling us in the process."

Later that night, German guards made a point to tell the American prisoners that most of the town had been leveled in the air attack conducted by more than fifty bombers, and that the first reports indicated at least four hundred had been killed in the attack. While the three prisoners sensed the anger in the guards, they also could see the fear in the Germans' eyes. Tim wondered, *Are these guys losing faith in Hitler? Are they thinking the end is near?*

Saturday, 24 December 1944
Camp Patrick Henry, Newport News, Virginia

Michael and the rest of Sergeant Wright's platoon were breathing hard after their ten-mile run. While that distance at Camp Swift had become routine in the dry air of Texas, running ten miles in the humidity at sea level somehow seemed tougher. Or maybe the two-day train ride had an impact. Or maybe it was excitement that the division was getting ready to deploy that caused their breathing to be more labored. In any case, the good sergeant did not want his men to have much free time to worry about the future.

Ever since their train pulled up into the camp's train station two days earlier, Michael and those with him marveled at all the activity around the confines of Camp Patrick Henry, named for that revered Revolutionary War hero. As one of the major staging areas designed specifically to deploy units to Europe over the last several years, Camp Patrick Henry's personnel played a major role in moving six Infantry divisions and one Armored division, each made up of close to fifteen thousand soldiers, to the European theater. And now the 10th Mountain was next in line.

Wright gathered his platoon around him as the men cooled down after their run. "Good run, men. Since a few of you are recent replace-

154

ments, you'll have to catch up quick because we're gonna keep our running up to snuff every day for as long as we're here, and yes, tomorrow as well, and yes, I know tomorrow is Christmas. Get used to it. There will be no holiday breaks where we're going. Now, let's get down to business. First, whatever I tell you today stays here. Don't write anything in your letters to your girlfriends, mothers, fathers, nobody about what I'm about to tell you. Understand?"

The sergeant watched as all of his men shouted back, "Yes, Sergeant."

"Good. Now here're the facts. The 86th Infantry Regiment boarded the *SS Argentina* on December 11 and arrived at their intended port two days ago. It appears right now our regiment and the 85th Regiment will leave here in a week or so. That, men, is why we won't slack off one bit on our physical training. You are restricted to this camp. Have a beer or two while we're here and get some sleep because once we get to our new location, there won't be much of either one. Now if there are no questions..."

Seeing a hand shoot up, Wright growled, "Yes, Van Ostenburg. I can always count on you to ask a question. What is it?"

"Sergeant Wright, you never said where we're going. Where's this mysterious port the 86th landed at?"

The sergeant smiled and gave an answer that delighted all his soldiers. "Guess I forget to tell you, didn't I? Naples, Italy."

Late Sunday afternoon, Christmas Day, 25 December 1944
The Van Ostenburg home, Grand Rapids. Michigan

"Wish Paul and Eleanor could've made it. They're so close."

"Well, that's true, Mom, but like Paul told you, he's on duty this weekend and that's just the way it is. Look at it this way. He's a whole lot safer in Illinois this Christmas than he was in India last year at this time."

155

"Yes, you're right of course, but..."

"No buts, Mom. There are a lot other mothers who would trade plac-es with you right now and you know it."

"OK, Jay. I've got it. You're right." Margaret sat still for another mo-ment before a big smile came out. "Well, now that I have been officially chastised by my son, I think, Jesse, it's time you and I clean up this table and hustle these men out of our way. I'm sure they can find something to talk about. As for me, since you've delivered such great news that I'll be a grandmother in six short months, we need to talk about decorating rooms and things I can buy to help spoil my first grandchild."

****

"Glad to know, Dad, that Paul's thinking about accepting a commission. You think this means he'll be making the Air Corps a career?"

"Sounds like it to me, Jay. Could do a lot worse. Seems to be the right thing for him. Couldn't be more pleased for him."

"Well that's good. But he'll have to learn like I did that there's a dif-ference between the officer way to get things done and the NCO way."

"Don't think I've ever heard that phrase before. What do you mean?"

Jay laughed, "Come on, Dad, think about it. The officer solution to most problems is accomplished with a lot of show and a lot of detailed instructions, spending way too much time telling someone how to build the watch instead of telling them what time it is. The NCO technique is more along the lines of the shortest distance between two points is a straight line. And doing it all without a lot less fluff or unnecessary instructions which tend to bog down the whole process."

Ben chuckled, "Now that you say that, I know exactly what you mean. The officer way and the NCO way. I'll remember that. And yes, as I think about it, the NCO way works a whole lot better most of the time. Tracks pretty well with something I heard a wise old First Sergeant tell his brand new company commander one day. 'Captain,' the First Sergeant said, 'you may command this company, but I run it.' The first shirt wasn't being arrogant or disrespectful. He just wanted to teach the young officer that his NCOs could handle a lot of the details so the captain could concentrate on the big stuff."

The two men sat still for a long time before Jay looked at his father. "Jesse and I took a drive over to Ann Arbor a few weekends ago. When we got there, we went by Betty's place. She answered the door but was very evasive. She said she was real busy and that we caught her at a bad time. Didn't invite us in so we talked with her outside on the steps for maybe ten, fifteen minutes before we excused ourselves and came back home. Something's going on there. Can't tell you exactly what, although I've got my suspicions. Just not sure I want to voice them."

Ben nodded. "I think based on that, I'll try and check a few things out without disturbing your mother. I may require some help from you, but for now, let me see what I can find out."

Late Sunday afternoon, Christmas Day, 25 December 1944
Camp Patrick Henry, Newport News, Virginia

The Christmas meal was better than expected, particularly since the number of men to be fed in the chow hall that day was staggering. The turkey and ham were cooked just right, along with the sweet potatoes and all the trimmings, including cherry pie. Since Michael had gone to the Christmas Day service at the nearby chapel, it felt like Christmas even if there was no snow on the ground. And with the news about the unit's expected departure, he thought it best to write a letter to his folks.

...It's Christmas Day and after a good meal from the mess sergeants, we're resting

up. Expectations are that we'll be shipping out soon. Of course, I can't tell you where or when but please pray for us. After all this time of training all over the place, we're ready to go. We've got great leaders and as the saying goes, "we're all leaning forward in the foxhole." I'll write again when I can but don't know when that'll be.

Your loving son, Michael

As he reread the letter to himself, his bunkmate, George Middleton, strolled into the drafty wooden barracks building that served as their temporary home. "You're doing the same thing I did. Figured I'd better send the folks something now. No idea how long it'll take a letter to get from Italy back here. You all set and ready to go?"

"Yeah, think so. I know my body is. But I suspect like 'most everyone else, I'm wondering how I'll react to gettin' shot at for the first time. And I wonder, too, what it'll be like to shoot at another man."

Middleton said nothing for a long time as he sat on the bunk bed next to Michael. "Yeah, I've been thinking about some of that, too. I just don't want to let you or anybody else in the platoon down. We're brothers. Not like flesh and blood brothers, but something much deeper. Hard to explain, but we've been through so much together."

The ex-logger rubbed his cheek before he finished his thought. "I know you better than I'll ever know my flesh and blood brothers. And I trust you more. Like I said, just want to make sure that when the bullets start flying, I don't let you down."

0600 hours, Wednesday, 5 January 1945
Southeast of Mainz, Germany

Somehow the two German soldiers managed to stay alert with their backs up tight against the rear gate of the truck as it bounced along the narrow, rutted road. They said nothing to the three Americans who were curled up next to each other trying to conserve heat and get some sleep at the same time.

Finally, after almost a six-hour drive, the three-vehicle convoy came to a halt, giving both the prisoners and their guards a chance to stretch and relieve themselves along the deserted road an hour before daybreak. And because of the freezing temperatures, it was not too long before the prisoners and the guards stood around several small, sputtering fires trying to warm themselves, smoke billowing from each of the fires because of the wet wood they had used for fuel.

"Any idea where we are, LT?" Tim Van Ostenburg asked under his breath as he wrapped his threadbare blanket around his body.

"Been watching real close through the cracks in the tarp and as the guard looked back from time to time. We're heading east, that's for sure. Lot of low hills around. Look over there. We're near some grape fields. Probably to make wine. And we know for sure from what that one German told us back at Trier, they're taking us to some stalag, east of the Rhine River. Since we haven't crossed any big bridge, I'm sure we're still west of the Rhine."

Richardson stopped talking when one of their guards walked over to the Americans, giving them some water along with some bread and cheese before he returned to the larger fire where his friends warmed themselves.

The pilot then lowered his voice again. "From what I remember from having overflown this area a few times looking for some of the small airfields the German fighters use, I'd say we're south of Mainz. Got to be close to the Rhine as the river starts to make a bend to the south between Mainz and Frankfurt."

He looked around as the dawn sky grew lighter. "The terrain here seems real familiar to me. Can't be sure, of course, since that was a few months ago, that I was flying in this general area. Sure looks different from the air but..."

The *oberleutnant* in charge of the convoy noticed the brightening sky as well, ordering his men and the prisoners to put out the fires and board the vehicles. As they began to stamp out the flames and kick dirt on the coals, Richardson mumbled to Van Ostenburg and Thompson, "Go slow. Don't get in a hurry."

With those instructions issued, all three men stalled as best they could, taking their time tamping down the coals as the fires still gave off some smoke. When they had settled into the back of their truck a few minutes later, Van Ostenburg asked quietly, "OK. What gives?"

Richardson grinned, "You hear what I hear?"

"Hear what?"

"That rumbling sound that only comes from a Pratt and Whitney Double Wasp radial engine mounted on the front of a P-47 Thunderbolt. Flight of at least two birds not too far away. Probably looking for some targets of opportunity, like a train or a small convoy. I'm hoping those sharp-eyed pilots might be drawn to a little smoke. If they find us, and if you can get out of this truck in one piece, find a hole in the ground and pray."

****

Two minutes later, as the convoy approached a small hill with a grove of thick trees on top, the German officer suddenly gave the signal to his drivers to spread out and take cover. Just after the three prisoners leaped from the truck, it was blown apart by the eight 12.7 mm machine guns from the lead P-47. The second aircraft in the formation then made mincemeat out of the other two German vehicles as the pilot unleashed a long stream of armor-piercing and incendiary bullets into them.

Richardson hollered, "Get as low as you can and stay still. They'll make another pass at us if they see any movement."

Five minutes passed before the pilot stood up. "OK. They're gone. You two grab whatever gear and weapons you can from the dead Germans and then we'll head up to the top of this hill and get our bearings."

Van Ostenburg looked at the pilot. "It's just you and me, Joe. Townsend's dead. Took a round in the gut and one in the head. Never had a chance."

Richardson looked at the dead soldier for a few minutes before nodding, "OK. Like I said before, we'll gather what we can and then get up on that hilltop. We'll wait until nightfall and then come back and bury him if we can. I'll check out the officer. Should have a map with him."

Thursday evening, 6 January 1945
Fukuoka POW Camp, Number Seventeen,
Island of Kyushu, Japan

Even as the guards tried to hurry the prisoners along this part of the path that crossed one of the highest points for several miles, the prisoners slowed the pace. "Lots of smoke coming up from down south, LT. You think maybe our bombers are taking it to the big ships in Nagasaki again?"

Jim Van Ostenburg smiled as one of the guards shouted in butchered-up English, "Go now! Go now!" The officer made a slight bow before ignoring the guard's prodding. "That's what I'm thinking. If they are, that'd make what, the third time in the last seven days?"

As the guard became more insistent, the men moved a little quicker. "Yeah, I think so. I know these guards get pretty tight-lipped whenever they see our flyboys overhead or they hear some bombs tearing the daylights out of the homeland. A few of these thugs are taking out their frustrations on our guys more than usual. Guess after all this, we should expect it."

"Yeah, Johnnie, I think you're right. I know for me, every time I hear the sound of our bombers overhead, my morale goes up. It's like they're saying, 'Help is on the way.'"

"You got that right, sir...Oh, watch your six. Looks to me like *The Cobra's* got his sights on you. He's making a beeline for you. Be careful."

Jim stood still and steadied himself as the Japanese soldier drew closer, his limp now less pronounced. *The Cobra* faced Van Ostenburg, staring into his eyes for what seemed a long time. No words came from his lips nor were any blows delivered from his clenched fists. Finally, the soldier took a short step back, clasped his hands together, and bowed ever so slightly. He then did an about face and disappeared from where he came.

As he would recall many times in the years that followed, this was the last time Jim Van Ostenburg or any of the other prisoners saw *The Cobra*.

Two hours after dusk, Thursday evening, 6 January 1945
Southeast of Mainz, Germany

"Thanks for praying for him, LT. Think he'd like that. Not sure, but I think so," Tim said as he put down the shovel he found next to one of the demolished German vehicles.

"Yeah, well it's the right thing to do; burying him and all. Wanted to make sure I got his dog tags. Can't do the same for the Germans. We'd be here all night if we tried to bury all seven of 'em. Their own soldiers will find them soon enough. As for you and me, we got to make the best of the dark we got now."

"Makes sense. You got a good fix on where we are?"

"Yeah, I think so. That map and compass we found were exactly what we needed. Based on how we were traveling and knowing they wanted to get us across the Rhine, I figure we're about five, six miles west of Oppenheim, near this little village of Dexheim. Best thing we can do to not get picked up by the Germans is to stay away from any people we see, and to keep moving west. That's the direction our guys will be coming from sooner or later. You good with that?"

"Yeah. I'm with you."

"Alright. We'll move each night starting about an hour after dusk and find someplace to hole up an hour before daylight. Also, it's you and me together in this, so can the LT stuff. Like I told you before, name's Joe."

"OK, Joe, I got it."

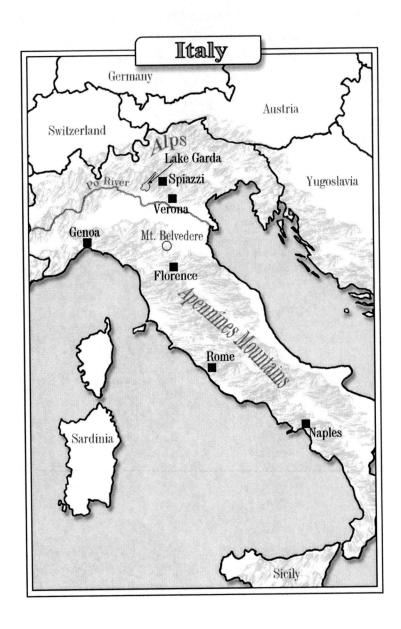

CHAPTER TEN

"GAVE PROOF THROUGH THE NIGHT"

World and National Events between
26 December 1944 and 19 March 1945

ALLIED FORCES DEFEAT GERMANY'S LAST MAJOR OFFENSIVE IN EARLY January 1945 and push the German Army back towards its borders. In the Pacific theater, US forces win bloody battles against the Japanese at Iwo Jima and in the Philippines. Meanwhile the bombing campaign against the Japanese mainland accelerates. Plans for Operation DOWNFALL, the invasion of Japan, are in full swing.

Late afternoon, Monday, 20 March 1945
Police Headquarters, Grand Rapids, Michigan

"I guess that wraps it up then. Who would have thought it possible? The Japanese trying to bomb the United States. Any doubts in your mind, Ben?"

"Nope. Not a one. I'm just glad we called the FBI right away about this. Got to wonder how many more of these balloons are out there somewhere. Sooner or later some kid somewhere is gonna happen on one of these things. Then they'll start pulling and tugging at the wrong end and it'll blow up in their face. I assume the FBI will be notifying all their offices about this."

"As far as I know. Might cause a real panic if I started calling a bunch of police chiefs."

"Yeah, that wouldn't be good. Best to let the Federal boys take care of it. How much did that bomb weigh anyway?"

"Thirty-three pounds. Could have done some real damage. All I can say is I'm glad for your help. When I first heard about this suspicious balloon with possibly Japanese markings, you were the first man I thought of because of all your experience in the war and all. I'm just glad the farmer who found this thing didn't get carried away and start moving it around. Could have been a bad day for him."

"No kidding. That was probably the best phone call he made — calling you so we could get the FBI to look at it."

"Well, I couldn't have done it without you, Ben. I appreciate your help. If I hear any more about this, I'll give a call. Thanks again."

"Glad I could help."

Ben walked down the steps of the Grand Rapids Police station and slowly drove his old beat-up car home. *How ingenious. Who would have thought the Japanese would send hydrogen balloons with baskets of explosives tied below across the Pacific Ocean, using the air currents aloft as the means of delivery, all to bring the terror of the war to American shores. Can't fault them for their ingenuity. Had to take some good planning. Also means we can't take them for granted either. I wonder how many more of these balloons are headed our way?*

Late afternoon, Wednesday, 22 March 1945
Behind a large haystack near a
German farmhouse, Dexheim, Germany

"Stay still."

"You sure they're our guys?"

"Yeah, I am," whispered Sergeant Tim Van Ostenburg.

"That red diamond on that jeep that just passed by means these guys are from the 5th Infantry Division. 'The Red Devils.' Our guys all right. Probably been in some tough fights. They're ready to blast away at anything that moves. So when we get up in a minute, you follow my lead. No weapons. Hands up. No sudden moves. You got that?"

"Gotcha.' Remember I'm just a dumb fighter pilot."

When Tim sensed the time was right, the two men slowly stood up with their hands held high as the next squad of American soldiers, weapons at the ready, began to pass their hide position next to the farmhouse. Tim wanted to hug each one of these soldiers, but with the odd mix of clothes he wore, he remained still, not wanting to be mistaken for a German soldier. Better to move slow and easy. Never could tell how trigger happy these "Red Devils" might be.

****

Tim sat quietly on the edge of the grove of trees where the headquarters element of the "Ramrods," the 2nd Regiment of the 5th Infantry, had established their command post. It was now almost dark. He and Lieutenant Richardson had been in American hands for almost two hours as the soldiers who found them questioned their authenticity and shuffled them back to this command post so the S2, the intelligence officer of the regiment, could question them to make sure they were not Germans soldiers masquerading as Americans. The tired-looking soldier watching Tim had given him some K-rations and water, but perhaps because of orders, he did not enter into any conversation. Nor did he move his finger too far from the trigger of his M-1 rifle.

Finally, after thirty minutes, a buck sergeant signaled Tim to follow him to a small tent up the hill. "You Sergeant Van Ostenburg?" asked the thin, tall captain who stood at the entrance to the tent.

"Yes, sir. That's me. 1st Battalion, 175th Infantry Regiment, 29th Infantry Division."

"I'm Captain Arnold, S2 of the 2nd Regiment, 5th Infantry. Since you and the man with you claim to be American servicemen, it's my job to make sure you're who you say you are and get you back to the States. Fair enough?"

"Yes, sir. Sounds good to me."

"Good. So start from the beginning. When and where were you captured?"

****

"...So then after you buried Corporal Townsend's body, what happened next?"

Tim closed his eyes and replayed those days back to the officer. "We tried to move west to meet up with you guys, but there were just too many Germans every which way we moved. Couldn't get around them. We decided then that our best bet was to hide out. This one German farmhouse was pretty isolated so we hid out in the barn attached to the back of the farmhouse with the cows. Was on some high ground so we could watch the roads. We were right on the outskirts of this small town, Dexheim."

"Any Germans around?"

"Didn't see any fixed positions there, but there was a lot of vehicle traffic along the main road. Like I said, we had a pretty good view of the road from a hole in the hayloft of the barn."

"Tell me again, when did you escape?" the captain asked as he continued to take notes.

"Mid-January or so. Dates kind of run together. Anyway, we had been in this barn for a few days when I got surprised early one morning. Was trying to wash some of the cow dung off my clothes when a woman came around the corner of the barn and saw me."

"What happened then?"

"Neither of us moved. Then, after she looked at my uniform, she asked in broken English if I was an American. When I nodded yes, she ran back into her home. Even though it was now close to daylight, when I told Joe what happened, we figured we'd better make a run for it. But just when we were almost out the door, the woman showed up again and stood in front of us."

The captain nodded for Tim to continue.

"Captain, to make a long story short, through her smattering of English and Joe's and my pidgin German, we found out that her husband, Sergeant Heinz Schmidt, was captured in North Africa. He's been in a POW camp at Battle Creek, Michigan ever since."

"Come on. How could you find out all that?"

"Because Captain, she showed us a bunch of letters from him. All on Red Cross stationary. Had his name on it and where it was sent from right on the envelope. And because of what he told her in this letter, about how well he was being treated and all, Frau Schmidt told us she would hide us out until you guys came along."

"And so that's why you two look so well nourished?"

"Guess so. She did feed us pretty good. Brought us cheese and some meat and bread after it got dark each night from then on. Her name is Isabel. She treated us very well."

"Anything else happen while you're hiding out?"

Tim stared at the dirt for a moment or two. "Four nights ago, we heard some kind of German command vehicle stop in front of the farmhouse. Was a big staff car with an SS flag on its bumper. Two men, probably some high-ranking officers, based on the cut of their uniforms, went through the front door of Frau Schmidt's home with barely a knock. At first we thought they were coming after us, but before we could make a run for it, we heard Isabel scream."

"So what did you and the lieutenant do?"

"We figured they were raping her so we slipped out of our hiding place. Killed the driver who was out front with our bare hands. Got his gun and went inside... Those two inside never heard us coming. They never had a chance. Afterward we stuffed all three of 'em in their car and drove it into a ditch a couple of miles away from the farmhouse and set it on fire. Then we ran back to the farmhouse and prayed you guys would show up soon."

Captain Arnold made a few more notes on his pad before he stood. "Sergeant Van Ostenburg, let me be the first to say, 'Welcome back.' Your story and Lieutenant Richardson's are right on the money. Good to have you on our side. Just so you know, our long range scouts saw you and the lieutenant burn that German staff car from their position about four hundred yards away. We wondered what that was all about and now we know the full story. Seems to me what you two did that night deserves some kind of medal, but I can't promise you anything like that."

As the captain was about to exit the tent, he turned. "You should know that elements of this division will be crossing the Rhine at Oppenheim in the next few hours. One of the officers you and Richardson killed that night was one of those in charge of the German defense of the river. Thanks for the help."

Late Thursday afternoon, 30 March 1945
The Van Ostenburg home, Grand Rapids, Michigan

Ben's day at the store had been quiet and uneventful, nothing more exciting than changing a few parts on several old radios. With Margaret attending a women's meeting at church, he took time to relax, intending to read the mail she had laid out for him. His excitement grew when he noticed that the first envelope was already open. A letter from Michael. What a blessing.

Dear Mom and Dad   *10 March*

We now have some down time which gives me a chance to catch you up on all that's happened. My regiment sailed from Hampton Roads, VA early in January, arriving in Naples, Italy in mid-January. Once we got here, our whole unit got ready to move to the Apennines Mountains in central Italy.

In mid-February we finally got into our first big battle. Got to tell you, it tested all our mountaineering skills as we attacked Riva Ridge and Mount Belvedere, taking those two German strong points in four days. The Germans weren't too thrilled with us being there and they hit us hard for a time, but we held on.

Then earlier this month we captured some other towns, which really put the Germans in a bind because we've cut off many of their resupply and communications routes. Like before, the fighting's been costly, but right now, we seem to have things going in our favor. Seems It's just a matter of time before we finish 'em off. Seems to us grunts that our unit is leading the way — maybe it's just unit pride but we feel that way anyway.

Want you to know, I'm in a great unit with great leaders. I can't say enough good things about my platoon sergeant, Sergeant First Class Wright. You'd like him, Dad. He leads by example. Uses the words, "Follow me" quite a lot.

Right now we're getting time to rest up. Had a bath yesterday for the first time in a month. Got brand new uniforms. Felt like a new man. Then last night we

171

*sampled some Italian wine and some of their food. High marks all around from
all our guys.*

*I'll write again soon. Just can't tell you when that will be. Don't worry. I'm
keepin' my head down.*

Love you both, Michael

Ben read through the letter again, surprised somewhat that the censorship process had approved the letter as written. He then sat back in his chair, thinking about the phrases "...Germans hit us hard...fighting was costly...," all code for the bloody battles that took place in some very rugged, unforgiving terrain. Even though the press gave major coverage to Patton, Montgomery, and MacArthur, Ben sensed the Italian campaign with those unforgiving mountains was a bloody, brutal one. Many men died on both sides, yet Michael and those with him persevered and now had been pulled offline to heal their wounds, take a breath, receive replacements, do some remedial training, and get prepared to rejoin the fight again. It was a cycle Ben understood.

Jay and Paul will also understand what he's saying, but I won't trouble Margaret with any of this unless she asks. She has enough on her mind right now. Not knowing about Jim and Tim, a grandchild on the way, and her latest doctor's report. No, there is no need to get into any of Michael's code words with her unless she really pushes me...

The doorbell's ringing interrupted his thoughts. Upon opening the door, a young man asked, "Are you Mr. Ben Ostenburg?"

"Yes, son. I am."

"Sir, I have a telegram here for you."

Ben stared at the fellow and then at the envelope he held in his hand. With reluctance and trepidation, Ben took the envelope and thanked the delivery boy. He then returned to his chair and stared at the paper for a few moments before he opened it.

****

When Margaret came home an hour later, Ben greeted her by thrusting a glass of wine into her hand. "Ben, what is this?"

"Just something I wanted you to have as you read this telegram we received."

"Well I'm not sure."

"Just humor me. Sit down and read it."

Margaret slowly walked over and sat in her favorite chair and looked into her husband's eyes as he handed her the small piece of paper, which she grasped tightly. Her eyes traveled across the typed words rapidly the first time before she read the message again, much slower this time. Then she looked up at her husband, her face flushed, tears running down her cheeks. "Am I reading this correctly? Tim is alive? He's in American hands? He'll be coming home soon? Thank God. Our prayers have been answered!"

****

Within the hour, Jay and his wife joined in the celebration as they burst through the front door of the home. "What great news," Jay shouted as he hugged his parents. "Any idea when he'll be home?"

Ben smiled. "Nothing yet. I suspect we'll be hearing something soon. Right now, all your mother and I can do is praise God for watching over him."

"Yeah, I'm with you on that. I'm sure he'll have some good stories to tell. Not everyone escapes from the Germans. And on that note, where's the wine?"

****

Later that night, Jay and Ben found themselves alone in the living room. "Thanks, Dad, for letting me read Mike's letter. Sounds like his unit has been through some tough places. Gotta be rough, going through all those mountains, one right after another. Least we know where he is... just wish we knew something about Jim."

Then after a long pause, he asked. "Anything new about Betty?"

"No, son. Nothing. And so for that reason, your mother and I are going to go over to see her folks in a few days. We called them and invited ourselves over there for a 'social call.' Hope we'll know how the wind is blowing after that."

"That's good. Oh, and on a different note, at Jesse's last doctor's appointment all signs were pointing toward one child, not twins, although who can really say. We could get surprised. Wouldn't be the first time that happened. Due date is around the first part of August."

Friday evening, 31 March 1945
Fukuoka POW Camp, Number Seventeen,
Island of Kyushu, Japan

"Did you see that glow of those fires to the east and the south last night?"

"Sure did, Lieutenant. Too far away to know what's burning, but if I liked to bet, I'd say our bombers are dropping incendiary bombs on the Jap cities. Got to be hell down there for those people. Can't say my sympathy level for 'em is too high, considering they started this whole thing. You know, Pearl Harbor and all."

Jim Van Ostenburg and his fellow POWs knew something was going on with the Japanese as their normal rations of food, bleak as they had been before, were becoming smaller and smaller. Even rice seemed to be in short supply. And their normal complement of guards had changed. Many of the regulars were now gone, replaced by both older men and some young ones, almost boys, whose enthusiasm against those they guarded reached new heights.

Sergeant Patrick must have been thinking the same thing as he looked around at the guards. "Had one of those young punks try and take it to me yesterday. Don't know where he learned English, but he was spitting out some trash saying that when our men invade Japan, they'd be met by every man, woman, and child, all armed with spears and shovels and everything they could find to kill our guys. What do you think, LT? Could he be right?"

"Can't say for sure, Johnnie, but we both know how fanatical these people can be. Maybe that's why we're gettin' less food. And it'd explain why we're not getting any more medicines in our infirmary to help out the guys. Could be they're stockpiling supplies for an invasion. Or maybe they're just running out. But you're right. An invasion by our guys will be a bloody battle on both sides, that's for sure."

"'Course, on the bright side of all this, sounds to me like our guys are getting close. And if our bombers keep firebombing their cities, that should help cut down on the number of Japs who will be waiting on the beach for our men."

Jim nodded. "True. But our bombing their homeland like we are might motivate them even more. Either way, the best thing we can do is to keep on surviving. Keep living. Keep dreaming for the day when we can see our families again. That's what's helping to keep me going, Johnnie. Being with my wife again."

Sunday evening, 2 April 1945
The De Boer home, Grand Rapids, Michigan

"Ann, John, good to see you. May we come in?"

The Van Ostenburgs stepped into the home that they had visited on only a few occasions. After being seated in the modest living room, they both declined any refreshments, choosing to give polite, yet short responses to Ann De Boer's attempt to make them at ease.

After a few uncomfortable minutes, Ben said, "Thank you for seeing us on such short notice. The reason we wanted to come over is because we haven't seen Betty in some time and we're worried about her. As you know, we love that girl like she's our own daughter."

It was Ann who answered, her voice trembling a bit. "We thank you for asking. She's... she's been very busy at Ann Arbor working at finishing her degree at the university."

Margaret nodded. "Well, that's good to hear. But as Ben said, we're curious as to how she's doing and how you folks are holding up as well. It's a difficult situation for all of us and we keep hoping to hear something soon, just like Betty does."

John looked at his wife for a long time before he finally spoke, his eyes focused down at his shoes. "I must say, we are glad you called. We do have some things to talk with you about that have been on our minds for some time. We just didn't know how to approach it." He shook his head. "It's not an easy subject for either one of us."

Ben stared at the man, but said nothing. *It's about Betty and Jim. Has to be.*

"John, we really shouldn't..."

John cut his wife off. "Yes, we should and we must, Ann. We have to get this out in the open. It's the right thing to do."

The man stared first at Ben and then at Margaret. "As we all know, Betty and Jim have known each other for a long time. Four years of high school and then a few years after that before they got married. When you saw one, you saw the other close by. Each smiling at the other. A match made in heaven. But as you know, these last three years have taken their toll on Betty. We've prayed as you have for Jim's return and we know many others have prayed as well, all hoping we would hear something, anything. With no word, official or unofficial, about whether Jim is alive or dead..."

Margaret's hand went to her face as tears began to run down her cheeks. Ann left her place on one of the big chairs and went to Margaret's side, putting her arms around her. Then she looked up at her husband as if to say, "Go on, John. Go on."

"In the first year that Jim was missing, as you know, Betty lived here with us. We saw her cry herself to sleep almost every night. And we cried with her. While we had never experienced what she was going through, we gave her all the comfort we knew how to give. Unlike your family, who has some experience with war, all the possibilities of what could happen to Jim kept Betty, Ann, and me on edge every day. It got to the point that we dreaded seeing a strange car traveling slowly through our neighborhood, thinking perhaps that it might be someone coming with a notification about Jim."

Ben nodded. "We understand how tough this can be. We live with the same thoughts ourselves."

John got up from his chair and stared out the front window. "During most of the second year, Betty withdrew, almost into a shell. While you saw her on rare occasions, she was at her best when she was with you. Always wanting to keep a stiff upper lip. But deep inside, she was dying. Withering away. Wouldn't eat. Lost weight. Hardly left the house. We wanted to help her every way we could, but we didn't know where to turn. We suggested she get out, find a job, take some classes at the university at Ann Arbor. We thought it would be good for her to be around folks closer to her age. To find something that might give her purpose and meaning while she waited for Jim."

Neither Ben nor Margaret said a word, each listening carefully to John's words.

"In the last nine months or so, we noticed a new vitality in her. Needless to say, we were pleased about that, but when we began to ask questions, we learned, much to our surprise and regret, that this revitalization of her spirit, this new spring in her step, was not due to some work or in any way related to her studies. It was because of another man."

Margaret gasped. "Another man?" She looked at Ann first and then at Ben. "Another man? Why that can't be. It just can't be. She's married to my son."

John returned to his seat, remaining quiet for a long time before he looked squarely at Ben. "Some industrialist who works at the Willow Run plant near Detroit. He's part of the group that oversees the production line that builds B-24 bombers. According to Betty, they happened to meet, began to talk, and then spend time together. Their relationship has now escalated beyond our control."

Margaret's head snapped up. "What exactly do you mean, John, 'escalated beyond our control?'"

"Margaret, please understand, by all the laws of our land, she is a grown woman. We cannot order her to do or not do something we don't agree with. Through this man's legal contacts, Betty is in the process of seeking an annulment of her marriage with Jim so she can marry this other man."

John De Boer kept his eyes on Ben. "We would have spoken to you earlier about this, but we just found out all the details in the last week or two. And we've been agonizing over this ever since. We love our daughter and stayed by her every step of the way as she faced the unknowns about Jim. We were summoning up the courage to call you, when you called us about coming over. Ann and I are ashamed and embarrassed. We have great empathy for you, but there seems little we can do at this point."

It was now Ben's turn to stand and stare out the front window as both Ann and Margaret held each other tight, their tears blending together.

"When my unit returned from France in 1919, after having been gone a little over a year, a man in my squad learned that his wife had left him for another man. She did not have the courage to face the soldier. Instead, she sent him a letter telling him what she had done. And so this soldier never had the opportunity to talk to her face-to-face. Last I heard, he was all right because, like it or not, war toughened him and taught him to expect the unexpected. I also learned later that this soldier's ex-wife had divorced her second husband sometime after."

The old soldier returned to his seat. After another long period of reflection and prayer Ben cleared his throat. "My reaction to all this is that when my son comes home, if he does, Betty should have the courage, the guts, the respect for Jim's service to his country, to face him and tell him what happened. She owes him that. I do not know what he will do, or say, or how he will react. But I do know it is her duty to tell him the truth."

Ben wiped the tears from his eyes. "That is all I ask. Between the two of you, please make sure your daughter honors my son's commitment to serve his country by looking him in the eye and telling him the truth. I ask for your word on that — that Betty will speak to him in person and not take the coward's way out by sending him a letter."

****

Later that evening, Ben listened and watched and heard Margaret cry herself to sleep. And while he felt deeply for his son, he harkened back once more to when he was sent to war. *Thank you, God, that my wife, this dear woman who is now suffering so, stayed faithful to me during my time*

179

of war. Thank you again that she stayed focused on caring for our family even while I was in harm's way. Thank you that through all the temptations and fears and worries, we both remained faithful to our vows, to our pledge to one another. Oh, sweet Jesus, thank you. Thank you. Thank you.

Monday, 1 May 1945
The Van Ostenburg home, Grand Rapids, Michigan

Margaret answered the doorbell since Ben was upstairs. When he came down, he found her passed out on the living room floor, her pulse rate weak, her breathing labored. A telegram lay on the floor next to her hand. Racing to the phone, he called for an ambulance, and as he propped her head up to help her breathe, he stared at the piece of paper on the floor.

Just as he heard the ambulance's siren in the distance, Ben, too, read the telegram. "It is with deep regret that the War Department wishes to inform you that your son, Michael..."

Late Monday afternoon, 8 May 1945
Butterworth Hospital, Grand Rapids, Michigan

Jay had made it a point to visit the hospital every day after work to look in on his mom and dad. As he rounded the corner in the hallway that housed the intensive care unit, he saw his father sitting outside her room, his head down, his fingers slowly twirling his wedding ring.

"Dad, do you hear the bells?"

Ben looked up, a thousand-mile stare in his eyes. "What did you say, son?"

"The church bells. Did you hear the bells? They're ringing all over town. The war in Europe is over. The Germans signed the surrender. The war in Europe is over, Dad."

Ben looked at his son with that far-away look still in his eyes. "That's good, son. Real good."

"But..."

"Jay, your mother passed away about ten minutes ago. The doctors did all they could do. Her heart was just not strong enough. All the events of the last few years have taken their toll on her. All her sons going to war. The unknowns of Jim's situation. The stress and strain of each of you in danger. And with Michael's death, it was all just too much for her. I'm sorry, son, that she won't be able to hold her first grandchild. She was so looking forward to that."

Jay sat down and put his arms around his father.

After a time of tears, Ben looked at his son once again. "She loved you, and she loved this country. She understood it was our duty to serve. She would not have had it any other way."

Chapter Eleven

"That our flag was still there"

World and National Events between 9 May and 14 July 1945

WITH THE ALLIED VICTORY IN EUROPE, TENSION MOUNTS ABOUT HOW Germany would be governed among the principle Allies—the United States, France, Great Britain, and Russia. In the Pacific theater, the United States wins the battle at Okinawa and turns its full attention to bringing all its full military might to bear against Japan's homeland as preparations for Operation DOWNFALL continue. Initial estimates of the loss of American lives for the invasion are 500,000 to 1 million men. President Truman settles into the leadership role he assumes with the death of President Roosevelt on 14 April.

Friday, 14 July 1945
Deshon Hospital, Butler, Pennsylvania

Ben was grateful that Tim and Jay had made the decision to accompany him on this trip. The telegram from the hospital requesting that he visit one of their patients came five days ago, but once he read the entire message, he would not have turned down this opportunity to return to the Deshon Hospital for anything.

As the taxi pulled up to the entrance, Jay commented, "Looks pretty much like it did when I left. Bushes still need trimming. Wonder if the food still tastes the same."

Ben smiled at his son. "I wouldn't know about the food, but I do know the doctors and the staff did a pretty good job on you, and I, for one, can't thank them enough."

"You're right there, Dad. A lot of good folks who work here really care. Before we go in, I've got to ask. Are you ready to hear about what happened to Michael?"

The father stopped at the front steps and looked at his two sons. "You men survived some harrowing experiences and your brother did not. Coming here is the least I can do to honor the desires of Michael's platoon sergeant. There is no way in the world I could turn down his request. Am I a bit uncomfortable about what I might hear? Yes. But I consider it my duty to be here and talk with a fellow soldier. And, if I haven't said it before, I want to thank you both for coming with me. Means a lot to me."

****

Sergeant First Class Wright looked up as the three men approached his bed. He tried to sit up, but with both his legs wrapped in bandages and in some device keeping them from moving, the attempt brought him too much discomfort. Ben noticed Wright's right arm was also heavily bandaged and held to the side of the bed with some restraints.

"You gentlemen the Van Ostenburgs?"

"Yes, Sergeant Wright, we are. I'm Ben, Michael's father, and these are two of his brothers." Putting his arms on his sons' shoulders, he gestured in Jay's direction first. "This fellow here is Lieutenant Jay Van Ostenburg, a veteran of the North Africa campaign. He spent a couple of months healing from his wounds a few doors down the hallway. This other guy is Sergeant Tim Van Ostenburg, a veteran of the Normandy campaign, a man who escaped from the Germans after being held as a POW for about six months. As for me, I was spent some time as an infantryman in France twenty-five years ago."

Wright looked deeply into the eyes of all three men for a moment. "Well, it's an honor to meet all you fellow soldiers. Always figured Mike came from good stock, but we never had much of a chance to get into the particulars. I'd shake your hands, but my right arm is still not moving too good. The docs say it will heal, but it'll take a little time. I appreciate you coming." Ben nodded. "Our honor to be here. The message the hospital sent me said you had something important to tell me and so I brought these two with me to hear what you have to say, that is, if it's OK with you."

"No problem there, sir."

"Good. Now, one thing before you tell us whatever it is you have to say. My name's Ben. You got that? And this is Jay and this is Tim."

"Yes, sir. I mean, yes, Ben. I got it. My friends call me Sam."

Before anyone could say another word two young nurses, both wearing second lieutenant's bars, came into Wright's area in the large ward room, one carrying a tray with four cups of steaming coffee on it and the other dragging in two chairs, setting them next to the one chair that was already close by Wright's bed. The nurse with the coffee gave them a quick smile. "Since it looked like you gentlemen were about to have some good man talk, we wanted to make you comfortable. Take all the time you need."

****

"...and so with all the successes we had at Torri Iussi and at the Po River crossing, all hard fought and hard won, we knew we had the Germans on the run. While there were a lot of rumors about the Germans surrendering, at our level, you know, the grunt level, the Germans seemed just as determined as ever to fight it out."

Sam put down the coffee cup and stared at his right leg. "Our battalion kicked off the attack to seize Spiazzi, a town north of Verona, east of Lake Garda, at 0330 on the 29th of April. The town was like so many others we had taken. A thousand places to hide in the bricks and the stone walls and the rubble. Every building a potential German strong point. And they were using all the tricks they knew.

"Since our platoon was down to about two squads, Mike was moving his squad around to the right of this one building while me and my guys were covering them. Once he and his guys got ten or fifteen yards ahead, they covered for us so we could leap-frog past 'em. Just as we almost got to some cover in the rubble in front of us, the Germans opened up on me and my guys."

Looking at his arm and legs, the sergeant closed his eyes for a moment. "They hit us good and hard. And in less time than it takes to tell about it, Mike and his guys began firing and charged up to get to our wounded. It was during this melee that Mike got hit. He died right there in front of me."

Sam cleared his throat and stared at Ben. "If he and his guys hadn't made that charge, I wouldn't be telling you about it today. That's what I needed to tell you, Ben. Your son saved my life and the lives of three other men with me."

Ben stood up and looked out the window behind Wright's bed, watching several of the recuperating soldiers hobble around the golf course, the sun shining down upon them. He stood there for several minutes.

"Sam, thanks for telling us what happened. As we all know, in combat, you do things sometimes without thinking too much about the consequences. Your only focus is on helping the men you serve with,

186

the men you have grown to love in a way that few others could ever understand. That's what soldiering is all about."

He turned back to face Sam and his sons as tears ran down his cheeks. "Gentlemen, we are blessed. We are blessed because we all have known such men, such warriors. God bless them one and all." Ben sat down again and closed his eyes. The others remained still for several minutes.

It was Jay who broke the silence. "So what are the docs telling you, Sam? When can you get out of here?"

"The legs are a bigger problem than the arm. Last time they said anything, they were talking about me staying here for maybe five or six months. Since I've been a soldier for a long time, I'm just praying that these legs will heal well enough that I can stay in the Army."

"Well, if for some reason that doesn't work out, you give me a call. I'm always looking for a few good men in my business."

"I'll keep that in mind, Jay. Thanks. I really appreciate that. One thing is for certain. As they were putting me on the ship to get me back here, there was a lot of talk about the 10th Mountain sailing to the Pacific to be part of the invasion of Japan. I know I won't be a part of that fight."

Friday evening, 14 July 1945
On a train traveling between Pittsburgh and
Grand Rapids, Michigan

"You both heard Sam talk about the 10th Mountain and other units that may be heading to the Pacific to finish off the Japanese. That dovetails with a short note I got from Paul the other day saying he might be heading that way, too, in some kind of support role."

Jay watched the lights of a small town they were passing through as he added, "That'll be a tough fight. As fanatical as the Japanese are,

I imagine their entire population has been brain-washed enough that they would fight to the death against any invading forces. Wish we could just bomb them into submission. Not sure there are that many bombs in the world to do that, but I sure wish we'd try that first. Guess we'll just have to wait and see."

As the train rumbled on, Tim looked over at his father. "Dad, I've got a couple things for you. First, when we get back to Grand Rapids, I'd like to borrow that old car of yours and head over to Battle Creek for a day."

"Well, I suppose we can work that out. That's what, seventy miles away or so? That old car should make it all right. All you got to do is find enough gas ration cards. What's so important at Battle Creek?"

"Remember that I told you about the German woman who hid me and Joe Richardson from the Germans?"

"Yes, of course. Must be quite a woman. I'd like to meet her some day and thank her."

"Well, that's why I need to go to Battle Creek. Fort Custer, specifically. Her husband is one of the 3,700 German POWs being held there. Got a buddy there who told me he'll help me meet this guy. Got to tell him about how his Isabel saved Joe and me."

"Good idea, son. Good idea. I'm sure he'll be pleased to hear what you have to say. You said you had a couple of things for me. What else you got?"

"Once I get back from Battle Creek, I'm going to take a train down to Charleston, South Carolina. Last time I talked to Joe, he's serious about the two of us starting a barbeque business down there. So I need to take a look at what he's really talking about. You know, I need to do a recon. Like you've said many times before, one look is worth ten thousand words."

Tim smiled. "Who knows? If it works out, maybe I can give my snow shovel to Jay. He can always use another one."

5:29 AM and 45 seconds, Sunday morning, 16 July 1945
In the Jornada del Muerto Desert,
thirty-five miles southwest of Socorro, New Mexico

Known to only the select few who were involved in the Manhattan Project, the first atomic bomb, under the code name TRINITY, was detonated on this early Sunday morning at a remote site, fifty-five miles north northwest of Alamogordo, New Mexico. Working in secrecy in several locations for years, among them Oak Ridge, Tennessee, and Los Alamos, New Mexico, and in several universities including the University of Chicago, Columbia University, and the University of California at Berkley, all under the direction of Brigadier General Leslie R. Groves, Jr. and physicist J. Robert Oppenheimer, the test of the prototype device with an explosive equivalent of twenty kilotons of TNT was a success. The shock wave of the explosion was felt one hundred miles away, producing a mushroom cloud that rose to a height of almost forty thousand feet.

The official press release issued by the Second Air Force that day stated:

"The commanding officer of the Alamogordo Army Air Base made the following statement today: 'Several inquiries have been received concerning a heavy explosion which occurred on the Alamogordo Air Base reservation this morning. A remotely located ammunition magazine containing a considerable amount of high explosives and pyrotechnics exploded. There was no loss of life or injury to anyone, and the property damage outside the explosives magazine was negligible. Weather conditions affecting the content of gas shells exploded by the blast may make it desirable for the Army to evacuate temporarily a few civilians from their homes.'"

0815 Hours, Sunday morning, 6 August 1945
Fukuoka POW Camp, Number Seventeen,
Island of Kyushu, Japan

Jim Van Ostenburg had been in the mine for about two hours, laboring along with the other men he was responsible for. Their task this morning, like all other days, was to bash the walls of the mine with their shovels and picks, breaking through the rock to find the coal needed by the Japanese. The morning had been uneventful until...

"LT, you feel that?"

"Yeah, I do and I don't like it. Earthquake maybe." Without a moment to lose, Jim shouted, "Get out! Run for it!"

Fearing a cave-in, all the Japanese guards and their prisoners sprinted for the mine's entrance several hundred meters away, the pathway lit only by some flickering candles notched in the wall every ten meters apart up the inclined tunnel. Although hunched over in their sprint because of the low ceilings, they all emerged into the daylight. While the slight shake was no longer present, a strange yellow glow in the sky far to the northeast captured the attention of the guards and prisoners alike.

"What do ya think it is, LT?"

"Johnnie, I'm guessing. Not sure. Could be a big bomb. Or maybe an ammo plant explosion. Or an earthquake. Just don't know." Inspecting the skies around them in greater detail, he added, "Funny. Don't see any of our bombers flying around like they have of late. Maybe they're just sleeping in a little longer today."

****

Although two days of leaflet drops on the city had warned of a heavy attack, and on the morning of 6 August 1945 a uranium fission bomb nicknamed "Little Boy," equivalent to fifteen thousand tons of TNT, was dropped by the crew of *Enola Gay*, destroying much of Hiroshima. Later that evening, three members of the Japanese Supreme Council of War voted to sue for peace. An equal number on that council voted to continue to fight. And so the war went on.

1100 Hours, Wednesday, 9 August 1945
Fukuoko, POW Camp, Number Seventeen,
Island of Kyushu, Japan

"Sure is hot down there today, LT."

"Yeah, it is, Johnnie. Glad they're giving us a break to come up above ground to catch a breath of some fresh air for a few minutes. Look at that sky. Some big clouds, but still some pretty blue up there. Would be nice to work above ground for a change."

As Van Ostenburg scanned the sky above, he thought, *Wonder where our bombers are today? Some days we see a lot of them and other days, nothing. What does that mean?*

"Yeah, sure would. Could work on my tan. Whoa!... What's that?" the sergeant shouted as he involuntarily ducked behind a nearby rock as a bright flash of light burst from the south.

In seconds, all the men around them, Japanese and Allied soldiers alike, hit the ground. Soon a huge, mushroom-shaped cloud rose in the distance, causing many to instinctively keep their heads down from the blast that occurred fifty miles away. As the noise, the rumble of the ground, and the bright light began to finally dissipate, Van Ostenburg was not the only man to wonder, *God, what have you done? What have you given to mankind?*

And as the men looked south toward what they believed to be the

191

port city of Nagasaki, many wondered what it must have been like to be the target of such destruction.

Johnnie looked over at Van Ostenburg. "What is it? Some kind of super bomb?"

"I can't tell you that for sure, Johnnie. Let's pray it is."

****

Kokura was the primary target that morning, but when that city was obscured by clouds, the crew of *Bock's Car*, the B-29 carrying the plutonium bomb with a blast yield of twenty-one thousand tons of TNT, diverted to its alternate target, Nagasaki.

The Japanese government still wavered in its decision to give up for an additional five days, until 14 August, when the Emperor of Japan signed an agreement to surrender, sending messages through Swiss diplomatic channels to the Allies. The official date of Japan's surrender was 15 August 1945.

That evening, President Truman announced Japan's capitulation to the American people. In part, he said,

"This is a time of great rejoicing and a time for solemn contemplation... I think I know the American soldier and sailor. He does not want gratitude or sympathy. He had a job to do. He did not like it. But he did it. And how he did it!... On this night of total victory, we salute you of the Armed Forces of the United States — wherever you may be. What a job you have done! We are all waiting for the day when you will be home with us again."

Formal documents were signed by Allied and Japanese commanders in Tokyo Bay on the deck of the battleship *USS Missouri* on Saturday, 2 September 1945.

Early morning, Saturday, 19 August 1945
At the former Fukuoka, POW Camp, Number Seventeen,
Island of Kyushu, Japan

The plane, a B-29 Superfortress, made a low-level pass over the camp, wagging its wings up and down as it passed over the compound. Then the huge bomber rose higher, and on the next pass, four paratroopers could be seen drifting to earth under their white parachutes.

When the men hit the ground, they were surrounded by the former prisoners of war. After a few minutes of smiles all around, the leader of the paratroopers asked to meet with the Allied leaders, of which Jim Van Ostenburg was most junior by rank.

****

The Army major studied those around him, most of them skin and bones, the result of malnutrition and sickness for a prolonged period. And since the major was a doctor he was not surprised that many exhibited the classic signs of beriberi: difficulty in walking, loss of muscular function, and vomiting. His job was now to give these men hope and begin the steps for a quick, safe return to their homelands.

"Gentlemen, as I'm sure you have figured out, the war is over. The Japanese have surrendered. The formal papers will be signed within several weeks. Until then, it's my job and that of my team to assess your medical and physical needs and get you ready to go home as soon as possible."

The cheers of joy from the men around him went on for several minutes. Tears ran down the cheeks of all the former POWs, many of whom like Jim, had been held captive by the Japanese for over three years, while some of the British and Dutch POWs in the camp had been held for closer to four and five years.

"Supply ships are now being prepared to head our way. Even though Nagasaki was hit hard by our second atomic bomb, our ships will dock there in a week or so. Until then, we will be calling in aircraft to drop in all the supplies we need by parachute. My men have already called our headquarters and we expect the first of these drops within the hour. To help us get organized, what I need from you leaders is the number of men you are responsible for so we can get the right amount of supplies here."

Someone called out. "Major, we hear that, but the bottom line for our men will be, when will we be headed home?"

The major smiled. "Somehow I knew that question would come up. The most honest answer I can give you is that you'll know when I know, though I suspect you will be given priority." And then other questions came, one right after another. Thirty minutes later, Jim and the other leaders gathered their men in small groups to pass on the information they had received.

****

"...That's right. We'll be leaving Japan by ship in the next few weeks, most likely going to Manila where the medical docs will check us out really good before we head home."

"...Yes, we'll be able to send telegrams to our families from Manila. Starting later today, we'll be trying to get an accurate accounting. You know — your full name, rank, serial number, and such. We will also get a separate list of those we know didn't make it. As you can imagine, we want to be as accurate as we can about that so proper notifications can be made to the families back home as soon as possible. After all these years, I think we can all appreciate what they've been going through."

"...Back pay? Not sure about that, although I do know that each of us will be advanced in grade by one rank. So congratulations. If you were a corporal yesterday, you're a sergeant today."

"...Yes, you heard right. Our guys dropped two "A" bombs on the Japs. One on Hiroshima three days before the one we felt when they dropped it on Nagasaki."

"...That's right. From what I was told, both cities were leveled. I'm sure at some point we'll hear a lot more about the devastation those bombs caused."

"...What do I think about that? For me, if dropping some big super bombs helped bring the war to an end and save American lives, you bet I'm OK with it. And if you figure those bombs helped bring the war to an end, they probably saved a lot of Japanese lives as well."

"...Yeah, I asked that same question. The major didn't know the exact numbers, but he thinks there are around thirty to forty POW camps spread around Japan and other places they still control in Korea, Manchuria, China, and Indochina. Besides soldiers from all the Allied nations in those camps, there are also some missionaries, nurses, and the like held in those camps also."

****

Late that afternoon, Jim took a walk to the top of the nearby hill outside the compound, something he had not been able to enjoy since his capture. Staring across the peaceful terrain in all directions, he breathed in the cool, clean air. He watched the birds fly, realizing that like them, he, too, was now free. He had survived. Kneeling down, he prayed, *Thank you, God. Thank you. You have made it possible for me, and many others, to now be free again. You answered our prayers. We leaned on you for our survival and you have brought us through the fire. We ask also that you wrap your arms around all those families whose loved ones are not coming home.*

Please bless them and uplift them... And Lord, I look forward to reuniting with my wife and with my family. Thank you for blessing me in that way.

Tuesday, 20 September 1945
The Van Ostenburg home, Grand Rapids, Michigan

"Hey, Dad. What can I do for you?" Jay asked as he answered his phone.

"Jay, I just received the best news. Your brother will be leaving Manila in four days. First stop, Los Angeles."

"Great news, but I've got to ask. Does he know about Betty? Any mention about her?"

"Yes, he said in his message that he'll be meeting Betty there. And since I heard from Betty's father earlier today, that now makes sense."

"I don't understand."

"Betty will be traveling by train to Los Angeles in the next few days to meet Jim at the same hotel where they last saw each other four years ago."

"Any idea about what will happen?"

"No, son, I don't, but I'll be praying for both of them. That's the best thing I can do. Oh, and I do have some other news to give you. Joe Richardson's family got news about his brother."

"And..."

"Not good. Tim got a call from Joe early this morning. Joe's brother was killed at Corregidor just before it fell in May of '42. After such good news that we have about Jim's safety, I feel for Joe and his family. When I hear things like that, it reminds me about how blessed we are, regardless of what happens between Betty and Jim."

Tuesday, 26 September 1945
The Hightower Hotel, Los Angeles, California

Jim smiled as he gave the taxi driver a big tip for getting him from the airport to The Hightower so quickly. The cab driver, an older man with graying hair, gave Jim a friendly nod. "Thanks, Captain. My best to you and your wife. Good luck."

The officer smiled as he turned to walk into the ornate lobby of the hotel where he and Betty spent their last four days together before his ship sailed for the Philippines not quite four years ago to the day.

As he approached the front desk, he spied the love of his life standing near the entrance to the coffee shop, her long blonde hair the color he remembered, her shapely figure still the same. As he rushed to her side, he grabbed her hands in his and looked into her eyes, his days of captivity now in the past. "My God, you're beautiful," he whispered as he held her tight.

Yet in the midst of his joy, something didn't seem quite right. The vitality and vigor he longed for in their embrace lacked the spirit he anticipated.

When he stepped back to look at her, the smile he remembered was only a shadow of the past. Betty looked up at him. "Jim, you look good. Far better than I imagined after all these years."

"Well, I'm feeling good. Two weeks of good food and the bright sunshine of Manila sure have helped. But enough of that. Come with me now, Betty. I called the hotel manager from the airport. His staff has our room ready. It's the same one we used the last time we were here. Come with me now so I can look at you. It's been so long."

"I can't, Jim. Not now. I have a place in the coffee shop in the corner reserved for us." And without another word, she turned and led the way into the restaurant.

Once they were seated across from each other, Jim blurted out, "I

197

don't understand. Betty, what is it? I know it's been four years for both of us. I know we can take our time."

"Jim, it's not that."

She stared out the window for a brief moment, summoning up the courage to give the speech she had practiced many times. "Jim, you were gone so long. I heard nothing about you. I didn't know if you were dead or alive. The first year, I cried myself to sleep every night. There were times that I wished I had been carrying our child, but then later, I was glad I wasn't. Then the second year I was lonely, so lonely. Then I went to Ann Arbor and began studies to become a grade school teacher. Things were going well for me and I felt better about myself and then... then I met another man."

Betty's voice fell to a whisper. "He was there to listen to me. By then, I had lost all hope that you were alive. I had no way of knowing. All the reports about how the Japanese brutalized you and the others, I gave up. And as time went by, I... I fell in love with this other man."

Now it was Jim's turn to stare out the window, watching the streets filled with people walking by, thinking about the men he had grown to love in several of the darkest places on earth. And about how he had survived, longing to be with this woman who now sat across from him.

"Betty, I still love you. I can understand how you must have felt. Four years is a long time to wait. But we can move past that. We can start our life again. I know we can. Just tell me you'll try."

Betty's eyes drifted downward, her voice soft, but firm. "I can't, Jim... I can't... I'm married."

"Yes, of course you are. You're married to me."

"No, Jim. I'm not. Not any longer. Our marriage was annulled three months ago. I am now remarried."

"But Betty..."

"No, Jim. It wouldn't work. Not now. Not anymore. I'm pregnant."

The soldier stared at his ex-wife for the longest time, remembering her smile and the sparkle of her eyes when she laughed. He thought of the way she flipped her hair, the way she touched him, and of the secrets they shared. *It took courage for her to come here to tell me the truth face-to-face. How embarrassed she must be. I wonder what I would have done if our roles in this tragedy had been reversed? Could I have been faithful for all those years, alone for so long, no word of any kind about the fate of my loved one?*

"Betty, you are a good woman. I wish you all the best. I have you to thank for saving my life. It was the memories of you that gave me hope every day for these last few years. For without that hope, I'd probably be dead."

As he stood up, he thought of Sergeant Ramsey and Chaplain Ken Thomas and others he had served with who would not be returning home. *I am one of the fortunate ones. One of the lucky ones. Thank you, God.*

"Goodbye, Betty." And with those words, Captain Jim Van Ostenburg walked out the door.

Tuesday, 3 October 1945
Kent County Airport, Grand Rapids, Michigan

Ben, Jay and Jesse with their newborn son Steven, Paul and Eleanor, and Tim watched Jim's plane land, and when he came down the steps from the fuselage, they mobbed him. And as could be expected, the event was appropriately reported and photographed by the staff of the city's newspaper, *The Grand Rapids Press.*

When they arrived home, Ben's church members had made sure the house was filled to capacity with food of every description. The family and neighbors huddled around Jim, peppering him with question after question, as he in turn asked about the details of their lives, particularly about the new members of the family: Jesse, Eleanor, and baby Steven.

As the day began to wind down, and the visitors excused themselves and the women moved their conversation into the living room, the five men settled into some weathered wooden chairs on the small back deck where they could enjoy the splendor of the stars awakening above them as the sun settled below the western horizon. First Jay, then Paul, and then Tim gave Jim short accounts of their experiences of the last few years, and like most soldier stories, their tales were a mix of the serious and the outlandish, the sobering and the humorous.

Ben looked at Jim. "You have much to absorb, son. Whenever you're ready to talk, we'll be ready to listen. No need to press you now. There's plenty of time for that."

"Thanks for understanding, Dad." He looked around at his brothers. "There is much to tell, and like you said, I'll get to it in time. Most of it, anyway. You all just need to know that I knew you were praying for me. I could feel it."

He paused for a moment to gather his thoughts. "And although you haven't asked, I know the question. Betty and I are no longer married and there is no hope for reconciliation. I have made peace with that in the last few days and I'm moving on. I can assure you that it will not weigh me down for the rest of my life. As we all know, war teaches us many things. Like you told us, Dad, even when all seems lost, the sun will still rise in the east, and because of that, it brings us hope every day."

As each one of them pondered the wisdom of that, Ben stared up the stars above as he thought about his dear wife. "What can we do for you right now?"

Jim laughed. "Well, if it's OK with you, Dad, I'd like to sleep in a real bed in this house tonight. And after some breakfast in the morning, I want to know about Mom and Uncle Bud."

"Yeah, I think we can handle that all right."

"After I met with Betty and found out what was going on there, I stayed in Los Angeles a few extra days to get my head right. While I was there, I made a few phone calls, and then stopped in Chicago for a day before I flew here."

"Why Chicago?"

"During my time at Camp O'Donnell, a POW camp in the Philippines, I got to know an Army chaplain by the name of Ken Thomas really well. As the weeks turned into months, and the months into years, God spoke to me through this man. I became convinced that I, too, should consider becoming a chaplain. After Ken died, it was as though God was telling me I was to take his place in the chaplaincy — that is, if the Army will take me."

"And?"

"As Tim knows, the Army cuts former POWs some slack in some areas, and so the Army has agreed that I can apply to be a chaplain once I complete the required coursework in an accredited seminary program. My stop in Chicago was to follow through with that. I'll start auditing some courses at Moody Bible Institute in three weeks, so I can officially enroll as a student in January. If I keep my head about me, I can apply to the chaplaincy in two years or less, depending how quickly I can move through the necessary courses. The GI Bill will pay for most of what I need."

Ben nodded. "Your mother would be proud." As he looked about, he pointed at Jay. "Jay, I think this news calls for a toast. Fill all these glasses with some more beer."

CHAPTER TWELVE

"OH, SAY DOES THAT STAR-SPANGLED BANNER YET WAVE
O'ER THE LAND OF THE FREE AND THE HOME OF THE BRAVE?"

Christmas Day, 25 December 1946
The Van Ostenburg home, Grand Rapids, Michigan

The wonderful sounds of laughter and joy were music to Ben's ears. To have his children and their families gather under one roof was a blessing for him. Even though he had considered selling the home he enjoyed for so many years with Margaret, he was pleased he had not done so. This was where he belonged. The good memories far outweighed the bad.

After finishing off the homemade pecan pie Jesse had prepared, Ben announced, "Today, I propose we start a new family tradition on Christmas Day. Let's go around the table and we each can tell the others about how we have been blessed in this last year. And, since I'm the oldest and this is my house, I get to make the rules. So, I'll go last. This means we'll start on my right and go around the table. Jesse, you're first, then Jay. Any questions before we begin?" And with that declaration, a new tradition began.

After Jesse and Jay mentioned how well Jay's canteen business was going, Paul and Eleanor surprised everyone when it came to their turn.

Paul winked at his wife before he began. "Well, we were going to tell you all later but now is as good a time as any." He stopped for a moment to clear his throat. "First of all, I'm getting promoted to captain in the next few months."

After shouts of congratulations filled the room, he said. "And there is more. Please hold your applause until the end. Second, we will be moving from Illinois to Greenville Army Air Base, in Greenville, South Carolina in the next few months. I'll still be part of the Eastern Technical Training Command and will be heading up an inspection team there. Eleanor and I want to complete that move by February if at all possible, because we found out last week that instead of expecting one addition to our family, there is a good possibility we'll have two bundles of joy arriving in late April or early May."

Ben grinned as he slapped his son on the back. "What wonderful news!" he shouted as the others joined in. "Tim, can you and Dorothy top that?"

"No, sir. Not even gonna try. But, I will say I am blessed to have married this wonderful woman six months ago, and even though she speaks with a bit of a Southern drawl, our lives in Charleston are overflowing with blessings. We have each other and our barbeque business is going well. And to give you all something to look forward to, next year for Christmas, we'd like all of you to come to Charleston and we'll treat you to some real, old-fashioned Southern barbeque."

After applauding Tim and Dorothy's invitation, Ben looked over at Jim. "Son, would you please tell the others what you told me?"

"I sure will, Dad. Be glad to." The oldest brother looked at his brothers and their wives, smiling at them. "What I told Dad last night was that my studies in Chicago are going very well and everything is on track for me to become an Army chaplain within a year; and before the cheers begin, let me hasten to add that when we eat Tim's barbeque next year in Charleston, I'll be accompanied by a woman named Sarah Osborne, although by then, her name will be Sarah Van Ostenburg. She's a wonderful woman I met in Chicago."

And with that announcement, tears and shouts of glee filled the room and a whole set of new questions began.

****

Later that evening, Ben and his sons gathered in the living room to enjoy some time together. "Got something I want to tell you. Something I've been thinking about for a while. Don't know if it'll work out or not, but within a year or so, I'd like to take a trip to Europe and visit the place where Michael is buried."

"Where is that exactly, Dad?" Jay asked.

"Florence, Italy. The official name is the Florence American Cemetery and Memorial. Forty-four hundred Americans are buried there, all from the Italian campaign. I got a notice a while back from the War Department giving me the particulars. Didn't know if any of you would like to go along."

"I can't speak for anyone else, Dad, but count me in," Jim said. "Just a matter of the best time to go. And of course, because of the dollars needed for such a trip, we'd have to do some serious planning."

Tim piped up. "I agree with Jim. I think we'd all like to go, but for me, when we go, I'd also want to see Isabel Schmidt and her husband. I owe that woman my life. And, if there was time, I'd also want to go and pay my respects to those from my unit who are buried at Normandy. I believe it's called the Normandy American Cemetery and Memorial. More than nine thousand of our brothers are there."

Both Jay and Paul also jumped on board. "Like the other guys, Dad, we're with you on this. Maybe not right away, but certainly within a year or two. Would you be OK if this trip you're thinking about was delayed that long?"

Ben's eyes blinked as he tried to balance his desires with the challenges and sacrifices his sons would have to make so that they could make the journey with him. If left to his own yearnings, Ben knew he would board a plane tomorrow, but with the possibility of his sons going with him, he was willing to put the trip on hold until they all could go.

"I see what you're saying and I appreciate it. You all have a lot of things going on. A move, a wedding, babies on the way, a graduation. As I think more about that, it would be best to plan way out. And as you said Tim, with some additional planning, I can look into visiting some of my old compatriots as well. Most of them are buried at the Meuse - Argonne Cemetery and Memorial."

"Any idea how many are buried there, Dad?"

Ben sat back in his chair and closed his eyes for a moment. "Over fourteen thousand."

Mid-afternoon, Tuesday, 17 December 1948
Greenville, South Carolina

Eleanor was tired. Paul had gone to the base early this morning to be with his three-man team as they monitored one of the crews while they conducted the pre-flight of one of the newer C-119 transport planes that would be flying later that day. Although Paul did not anticipate that he or his men would be flying today, they wanted to make sure the airplane was mission-capable. Soon after Paul left, Eleanor took the twins to the doctor for their eighteen-month check-up. While both girls were well within the norms for all the various measurements and checks the doctor and his staff performed, Jeanette, the younger of the twins by five minutes, had a bit of a cold. While the doctor was not overly concerned about that, for Eleanor, it was one more thing to keep an eye on.

From some strange reason, her stomach seemed in knots, but like most service wives, she had too much to stay on top of to be slowed down by a little discomfort. After putting the girls down for their afternoon naps, she made good progress on her ironing, until the ringing of the doorbell caught her attention.

Going to the door, she was surprised to see Mary Pearson, wife of Paul's commanding officer, and another woman who Eleanor did not know.

"Eleanor, this is Joanne Phillips, one of my neighbors. May we come in?"

"Certainly, Mrs. Pearson. May I offer you ladies some tea, or water?"

"No, thank you, Eleanor. Eleanor, there is something... something that my husband thought you should know."

"You mean Colonel Pearson?"

"Yes. It seems one of our aircraft is missing, and while we don't know have any details, there is some concern about its location. And it's possible that Paul and some of his team may be onboard."

"Well, Mrs. Pearson, thank you for stopping by, but there must be some mistake. Paul and his men were not scheduled to fly today. He told me they would be checking on this one crew and that he would be home around four. I mean sixteen hundred."

"Eleanor, that may have been his plan, but for some reason, it appears he and his men may have decided to go on the flight with that crew."

After a half-hour of meaningless small talk, Eleanor excused herself when she heard the twins start to wake up. When she returned to the living room with the twins in tow, Colonel Pearson and the base chaplain were in the living room talking quietly to the two women. The looks on the two men's faces told her everything she needed to know.

Unsteady and unable to see clearly, she sat down on the couch, and with soft tears running down her cheeks, she waited for the words she knew would follow.

Saturday, 21 December 1948
Greenville Air Force Base Cemetery, Greenville, South Carolina

While the afternoon sky was clear, the air had a nip to it. All of the brothers and their wives and children had arrived the day before to support Eleanor and Ben at the viewing at the nearby funeral home. And now, an even larger number gathered at the base cemetery to pay their final respects to Captain Paul Van Ostenburg.

The base chaplain was in charge of the short service, giving praise to God for the fine Christian witness that Paul was to many in his unit, and because of that witness, he quoted verse fifteen from Psalm 49: "But God will redeem my life from the grave; he will surely take me to himself."

The ceremony ended when Chaplain Jim Van Ostenburg read Psalm 23, which was immediately followed by the folding of the flag of the United States of America and the twenty-one-gun salute. The twins, who had been quiet until the rifles fired, began crying as they held their mother tightly. But then when the bugler began to play "Taps," the girls suddenly became still, mesmerized perhaps by the simple melody. Some would say later it was if the two girls understood the last, rarely heard lyrics of the bugle call: "To thy hands we our souls, Lord, commend."

There was not a dry eye among those in attendance when the bugler played the final note.

****

"Mr. Van Ostenburg?"

"Yes?"

"Sir, I am Colonel Jim Pearson, Paul's commanding officer. I just wanted to express my sympathies to you and the other members of your family. I apologize that I could not make it to last night's viewing. Others duties kept me from being with your family."

"Yes, I understand. Your deputy was there last night and he mentioned that you were deeply involved in the investigation and with helping the other families."

The colonel sighed. "Yes, I was. It will be some time before we find out exactly what happened. The C-119 is one of our newer planes, so with an accident like this, there will be a rigorous investigation, not only because of the aircraft, but also because of the men involved. With a crew of five and Paul and two others of his team onboard, the loss of so many good men is a tragedy in every respect."

Ben and his three sons who were close by could only nod.

"I have one of my best officers looking into the benefits Eleanor and the other families are entitled to. If at any time, Eleanor or any of you have questions or concerns that you feel are not being handled correctly, please do not hesitate to contact me."

Ben valued the plain-spoken words and the sentiment behind them. "Thank you, Colonel. I will pass that along also to Roy, Eleanor's brother. I'm sure he will also be a rock for her to lean on as well. He was a Field Artillery officer in the war and understands the system just as we do. And, Colonel, one more thing. We understand the responsibility that weighs heavy on your shoulders. Please know we'll be praying for you."

As the man walked away, humbled by the encouragement, another officer approached. "Sir, my name is Major Don Gaffney. I was stationed with Paul in India. I wanted to let you know he was a man of great integrity and courage. Did he ever mention to you about shooting down a Jap Zero?"

"No. He never said anything about that to me."

"One day two Jap fighters decided to pay our airfield a visit. After their first pass, Paul grabbed a machine gun and stood near the center of the runway, waiting for them to make another pass. I'm not sure why he chose that spot, but there he was—standing like a rock. When the Japs started their second gun run, he opened up on 'em. Within seconds, that first fighter was smoking and the second one pulled up and turned away. Not sure why."

"So what happened to the fighter that was hit?" Tim asked.

"It crashed at the end of our runway. And you know what? The Japs never hit us again. I think it was all because of what Paul did that day. Just thought you should know."

As the man walked away, Ben asked his boys, "Did Paul ever mention that to any of you?"

All three responded with a quick, "No, sir."

"He was a good man, your brother. A good man."

Tuesday, 1 April 1968
Arlington National Cemetery, Arlington, Virginia

As the first notes of "Taps" spread across the rolling hills of Arlington National Cemetery on this spring day, a soft, gentle breeze comforted those who gathered at the hallowed grounds to celebrate the life of another American hero. They listened to the bugle's piercing notes, their eyes filling unashamedly with tears as they watched the honor guard reverently fold the flag of the United States of America.

After saying their final goodbyes, the family slowly and quietly walked back to their cars and made their way to the Fort Myer Officers' Club. Colonel Jim Van Ostenburg had reserved several rooms so the family could have time to once more reflect upon the life of his dad before the family went their separate ways: Tim and Dorothy back to Charleston and their restaurant business and Jay and Jesse back to Milwaukee where Jay's business was booming. Since it would be some time before they could get together again, Jim did not want the day to end without having time with his brothers and their ever-growing families. And to have Eleanor and her husband Mac drive up from West Palm Beach, Florida, was also special.

Once he arrived at the reception, Jim realized for the first time how large the crowd was. He knew his family, of course, but who were all the others? And as he began to circulate around the room, he began to understand the impact his father had made on others.

The first man to come up to him was the Chief of Staff of the United States Army, General Harold K. Johnson. "Jim, the ceremony was a fine tribute to your father. I just wish that from all the times you talked about him, I could have had the pleasure of meeting him."

"Thank you, sir. He was a great role model for my family and me. I must say I'm humbled that you took time out of your day to come."

"Jim, as you know in your position as Deputy Chief of Chaplains, one of the most important aspects of our job here in Washington is to honor the service of men who have gone before us. While I thought I knew almost everything about soldiering, when you and I were in Korea fighting the Chinese, you told me one night over a cup of coffee about one of the lessons your father taught you, and I never forgot it."

"Sir, I must confess I don't remember."

"Well, I do. You told me about how your dad's unit did not give up. How they kept fighting even when they seemed to be facing insurmountable odds. How they still held on to hope. That lesson got me through some dark days then and continues to do so today."

General Johnson looked around at the crowd. "Jim, you have many to talk to so I'll be on my way. You still briefing me tomorrow on the state of our chaplains?"

"Yes, sir. My boss and I will be at your office at 0900."

"Good. See you then." And without another word, the Chief of Staff gave the man a quick smile and left the reception, his senior aide on his heels.

It was then that Jim noticed two older men talking to Jay and Tim in a most animated manner. He walked slowly in their direction, not wanting to interrupt them.

"...and they kept coming and coming. We killed plenty of those Krauts and, like Joe said, a number of our boys got it, too. But your dad, your dad held us all together. Even though he was shot up pretty good in his leg, he kept moving about, encouraging us, then shooting a Kraut who had gotten close, and then bandaging one guy up, and then he'd do it all over again. Four or five nights this went on. Never saw him slow down. Never saw him quit. Don't believe he got the recognition he deserved, but for those of us who were there and survived, we know what he did. Just wanted you men to know what kind of father you had."

After the two old soldiers moved off to grab some of the delicious sandwiches the Fort Myer staff had prepared, Jim asked Jay, "Lost Battalion veterans?"

"Yeah. They saw an article in one of the New York papers about Dad's death and so they drove down here last night. Before you showed up, they told us how he had gone out in front of their lines to pull back one of his men who had gotten killed. That's when he got shot. Trying to pull the body back into their lines. Never heard that before."

"No. Me neither."

As Jim looked around the room, he spied another face he had not seen in almost twenty-five years. He rushed over to the man. "Well, I'll be... Is that you, Johnnie Patrick? Is it really you? You've put on a few pounds, but I'd recognize that smile anywhere."

The former Staff Sergeant Johnnie Patrick hugged the man. And after a moment he stood back and looked at Jim. "Well, you've come a long way, Lieutenant, from being a half-starved POW to being a full bird colonel. What is this world coming to?"

"Yeah, miracles do happen. Good to see you, Johnnie. After all these years, what...?'

"I live down near Richmond. Used my GI Bill and have a nice little mechanic's business. And then two days ago, I saw something in the paper about a World War I hero passing away. And when I read the article, I knew it had to be your dad, and so I drove up here this morning to pay my respects. Always figured you came from good stock and I just wanted to tell you thanks once again."

"Thanks for what?"

"You kept me and a lot of others going during our time at Fukuoka. Without you keeping up our morale, a lot of men wouldn't have made it out of there. You did it, Jim. You did it. I'm proud to have known you. And now look at you. Heard you are getting promoted to brigadier general. They couldn't have picked a better man."

Jim's head dropped. "I appreciate what you're saying, but as you know, we saw a lot of good men die for no good reason. Wish we could have saved more."

"You did all you could do, LT. All you could do."

Johnnie Patrick looked around. "You've got a lot of folks to talk to, so I'll be on my way. When you get down toward Richmond, you look me up."

After the two men hugged once more, Jim watched Patrick work his way out through the crowd. It was then he noticed that both his brothers and their sons seemed to have disappeared. As he was about to conduct a search for them, he saw Eleanor's husband, Mac, standing alone.

"Mac, I'm glad you and Eleanor could make it here. It's good to see all of you. Those girls of yours have grown into two beautiful women."

"Thanks, Jim. Eleanor is a wonderful wife, and I've been blessed in many ways. First marrying her, then adopting the twins years ago, and being welcomed into this family. Though I can never take Paul's place, you and the rest of the family have always been most kind to me and I appreciate it. You've always treated me like a brother."

Jim smiled. "Well, even though you were a Navy Chief, you're a fellow warrior. A brother in our book. Did I hear Jeanette is engaged?"

"Yep. Marrying a young man who will be graduating from college next summer. Going through an ROTC program and so he'll be commissioned as a butter bar lieutenant on the day he graduates. Going into the Infantry. Good kid. His father was a B-24 bombardier in the Pacific during the war."

"Good. Glad to hear it. Have you seen Jay and Tim? I've lost track of them."

"Yeah. Believe they went into that small room in the corner a few minutes ago."

"Well, in that case, let's you and me go see what they're up to. Oh, and again, I appreciate you making the drive up here from West Palm. Long drive."

****

Jim and Mac found Jay and Tim holding court with their sons. Jay with his two sons, Steven, twenty-three, a recent OCS graduate, an Infantry officer who was on his way to Vietnam in the next month, and Benjamin, twenty-one, who was set to graduate from the United States Naval Academy in another year. Next to them stood Tim and his son, Joseph, nineteen, a recent graduate of Fort Benning's Basic and Advanced Individual Infantry enlisted training. Like his cousin, Joseph was expecting orders to Vietnam very soon. All the sons wore their uniforms proudly.

Jim smiled as he came into the room. "Is this a court-martial or just some kind of a male bonding exercise?" The young men reacted as they had been trained, snapping to attention.

"As you were, gentlemen. Today I'm Uncle Jim."

Jay grinned. "Glad you could join us, big brother. Actually, Tim and

I thought since we had a captive audience, we would pass on some of Dad's lessons learned before these guys head overseas."

"That's a good idea, and since I'm heading that way in a month or two for a quick visit, I need a refresher. So, if you don't mind, I'll listen in."

"Yeah, that's fine. Now as I was saying before my big brother and Uncle Mac came in, number one, even when it looks bad, never give up. Second, remember that God is always with you. And third, when the bullets start flying, do something. To sit on your butt and do nothing means you're gonna die."

Then it was Tim's turn. "Always be aware of what's going on around you. It's called situational awareness. Keep your head on a swivel. Keep looking around. Assume nothing. And remember, the enemy is not stupid. He's smart. He's looking for you just like you're looking for him."

Steven, the oldest cousin, glanced over at Mac "Uncle Mac, what lessons have you got for us?"

Mac, a man who had spent most of his time during World War II as a non-commissioned officer in charge of a 40 mm Bofors anti-air-craft gun on a Fletcher-class destroyer, stared at the young men for a moment as the opportunity to speak to them caught him off guard. It was not something he had thought about in a number of years. But he knew what needed to be said.

"Something I think that's true in the Army or the Navy. Don't be afraid of taking the initiative. If you see something that needs to be done, go do it. Like Jay said, to sit on your butt and do nothing gets people hurt. Think. Use the brain God gave you."

The three brothers then poured out more knowledge to the younger generation. "Always do your best... You hold the man's life on your right and left in your hands... A bad plan executed vigorously is always better than no plan at all," and other lessons learned just kept coming until finally, Joseph, the youngest one in the room, ventured into deeper waters. "How about you, Uncle Jim. What advice can you give us?"

While Jim had taught ethics and leadership and had practiced both for many years, he paused for a moment, thinking about what he could say to these young men that they could hold onto no matter what situation they might face, something that would be meaningful to them as they went to war. He thought about his mother and father, about the men he had served with, and about the men he had seen die for their country. He thought of what advice Sergeant Ramsey and Ken Thomas would give if they could.

"Two thoughts come to mind. First, each of you gave an oath to serve this country. You have given your word in front of God and men. So remember that. You have given your word. Let your word be your bond. Second, less than two hours ago we all stood on the sacred, hallowed ground of Arlington, surrounded by men and women who have served this country honorably. They did their duty, and in doing so, many of them died in combat. Inscribed on their tombstones are their names, ranks, places of service, and the decorations they earned. Each of those tombstones gives silent testimony about their love of country and love of freedom. They are all part of the great family of warriors within our country."

Jim paused for a moment to make sure he had their full attention. "And now you are part of that same family. A family of warriors. Men and women who run to the sound of the guns and not away from them. You have answered the call to serve this great country and have not used some excuse to avoid that call. You have decided to give your talents to your country rather than sit on the sidelines and watch others go in your place. For those reasons, I'm proud of you."

He then looked at his brothers before he spoke. "And lastly, let me just say this. Remember, you are a Van Ostenburg. We do not serve for riches or for wealth. We do not serve for fame or personal glory. We serve because it is our duty to our country. We serve for the common good. We serve because it is the right thing to do."

And with that, Colonel James Van Ostenburg snapped to attention and saluted the men before him as tears ran unashamedly down his cheeks. "On behalf of your grandfather, I salute you. We will always be a family of warriors."

AUTHOR'S NOTES

FAMILY OF WARRIORS IS WORK OF HISTORICAL FICTION, A GENRE that takes the facts history gives us and uses fictional dialogue around those facts to tell a story. As an author in this genre, I do not believe in changing history, nor is it my intent to do so. My purpose is to make history come alive for you, to make it breathe, to help give you, the reader, a more in-depth understanding of one time in history.

One of the purposes of *Family of Warriors* is to honor all those who have served our country through the years, and the families who steadfastly supported their family members. The idea for this work formed in my mind as a result of reading many works about the history of war, military biographies, and personal interviews, as well as through discussions with my relatives, other veterans, and their family members, coupled with listening to many old soldiers' stories. Research for this novel also included studying a great number of military history books and newspaper articles, blending that information into something that gives you a better feel for why many families in our country continue to serve this great nation, one generation after another.

Special mention must be given to several sources. First, the book *Days of Anguish, Days of Hope*, the story of Chaplain Robert Preston Taylor's ordeal as a POW in World War II, written by Bill Keith, helped launch my thinking about writing this book several years ago. In addition, interviews and discussions with Melvin Bessinger (now deceased) and Jack Ross of Grand Ledge, Michigan, added greatly to our story concerning POW experiences and about "Flying the Hump," respectively. Finally, newspaper articles and additional papers provided by Steve Van Oss about his father's experiences in North Africa were invaluable.

Historical Notes

The human cost in lives in World War II was staggering. Estimates are that 25 million died in the Soviet Union, almost 7 million in Germany, over 6 million in Poland, 15 million in China, and over 2 million in Japan. The total deaths worldwide during the war were 60 million.

During World War II, when the population of the United States was approximately 135 million, more than 16.3 million men and women wore the uniform of the United States—over 12% of our population. 400,000 died in the service of our country. In addition, 94,000 members of our Armed Forces were held by the Germans as POWs. Of these, 92,820 survived their captivity. This is contrasted with the 27,400 American service members held captive by the Japanese, of which only 15,000 returned home.

The Gold Star Mothers organization came into existence in 1928 to commemorate those sons or daughters lost in World War I. Today, the last Sunday in September is designated as Gold Star Mother's Day in the United States. Information concerning the current organization of American Gold Star Mothers, Inc. can be found on their website.

Blue Stars Mothers was formed in 1942 to help recognize and support mothers whose sons or daughters were members of the Armed Forces during World War II. During that war, the Matthees family of Goohue, Minnesota, proudly displayed seven Blue Stars: three for their sons serving in the Army, two for their sons serving in the Navy, and two others serving in the Army Air Corps. All seven of these men survived the war. Today this organization continues to support active duty personnel, promotes patriotism, and assists veterans' organizations.

Beginning in early November 1944 until early 1945, the Japanese launched 9,300 hydrogen balloons, called fire balloons or Fugo balloons, filled with anti-personnel or incendiary bombs attached with the express purpose of bringing the war to American and Canadian shores. The designers of these devices used the jet stream over the Pacific Ocean to deliver these weapons. Only three hundred of these balloons were ever discovered. In May 1945, the mother and five children of the Mitchell family were killed near Gearhart Mountain in Oregon when they accidently disturbed one of the downed balloons. They are the only known casualties of these attacks. Eventually balloons were found in eighteen states as well as in Mexico and Canada. The discovery of a balloon near Grand Rapids, Michigan on February 23, 1945 was the farthest east any have ever been found.

HISTORICAL PERSONALITIES

Sprinkled throughout *Family of Warriors* are several historical personalities. Below is a list of some of these men as they appear chronologically in our work.

General Omar N. Bradley. General Bradley was the Commandant of the US Army Infantry when the first Officer Candidate School class graduated at Fort Benning, Georgia in September 1941. Later, he commanded United States forces in North Africa and Europe during World War II, was Director of the Veteran's Affairs office, and then served as the Army Chief of Staff. He then became our country's first Chairman of the Joint Chiefs of Staff, serving in that position from August 1949 to August 1953. He is one of nine men ever to hold five-star rank in the history of the United States. He died in 1981 at the age of eighty-eight.

General Masaharu Homma. Lieutenant General Homma was the

commander of the Imperial Japanese 14th Army charged with seizing the island of Luzon during the attack on the Philippines. Although relieved of this command for not being aggressive enough in his taking of Bataan and Corregidor, he was convicted of war crimes for the atrocities that occurred on the Bataan Death March. He was executed by firing squad in April 1946.

Sergeant Jose Calugas. Sergeant Calugas received the Medal of Honor for his actions on 16 January 1942 in the Philippines as a member of the 88th Field Artillery. Later, after he was taken prisoner by the Japanese and then released, he fought as a guerrilla leader against the Japanese for the duration of the war. After the war, he became a United States citizen, settling in Tacoma, Washington. He died there in 1998 at the age of ninety.

Lieutenant Alexander R. Nininger Jr. Second Lieutenant Nininger was our country's first Medal of Honor recipient in World War II for his actions on 12 January 1942. The First Division of Cadet Barracks at West Point is named in his honor. He is buried at Arlington National Cemetery.

Brigadier General Paul Robinett. After recovering from leg wounds as a result of German artillery fire in the last days of the North Africa campaign, General Robinett spent the remainder of the war as Commanding General at Fort Knox, Kentucky, retiring from the Army at war's end. He then spent another nine years as chief of a special studies group in the Office of Chief of Military History arguing tactics. He passed away in 1975 in Missouri at age eighty-one.

General Jonathan M. Wainwright. A World War I veteran, Lieutenant General Wainwright was fifty-nine years old when he was taken captive by the Japanese at Corregidor. Like the other POWs, he suffered through many indignities. At war's end, he witnessed the Japanese surrender aboard the USS Missouri on 2 September 1945. Later he received the Medal of Honor for his actions as a POW and was then promoted to four-star general. He died on 2 September 1953. He is buried at Arlington National Cemetery

Colonel Ross J. Wilson. Colonel Wilson commanded the 1st Battalion 87th Infantry from December 1942 until the end of the Italian Campaign in June 1945. He later wrote *History of the First Battalion of the 87th Infantry*, a copy of which he gave me when I commanded that same battalion years later.

Major Asao Fukuhara. This camp commandant of the Fukouka POW Camp #17 was tried for war crimes in 1946 and was then later executed.

Lieutenant General Leslie R. Groves Jr. After the war General Groves was tasked with controlling all aspects of nuclear weapons in the US Armed Forces. He retired from the Army in 1948 and began working for Sperry Rand, an electronics firm. He died at the age of seventy-three in 1970. This West Point graduate is buried at Arlington National Cemetery.

J. Robert Oppenheimer. As a scientist, Oppenheimer spent much of his time after the war lecturing and discussing numerous scientific projects throughout the world. Diagnosed with throat cancer in 1965, he underwent a number of treatments to include radiation and chemotherapy. He died at age sixty-two at his home in Princeton, New Jersey in 1967.

General Harold K. Johnson. A stalwart warrior who fought in the Philippines in World War II, he was captured and held at Camp O'Donnell.

Later he commanded United States soldiers in the Korean War, and then later became the Army Chief of Staff from 1964 to 1968. In this last position he argued against our country's involvement in Vietnam and the tactics employed. He died in 1983 at age seventy-one. One of the men who served under him would later write, "He had an unusual sense of loyalty to the men under him, the kind of thing ordinary soldiers notice and value when they grade an officer."

The fictional characters in this novel were modeled and shaped by the thousands I have met who served our country in various capacities, men and women who daily exhibited valor and courage, honor and integrity. The characters in this book are a combination of many of those people. They are examples of what John F. Kennedy, a highly decorated United States Navy officer who served in World War II, spoke about in his inauguration speech on 20 January 1961 when he took the oath of office to become the 35th President of the United States:

"And so my fellow Americans, ask not what your country can do for you... Ask what you can do for your country"

ABOUT THE AUTHOR

ED DEVOS, A HIGHLY DECORATED MILITARY OFFICER, IS AN EXPERI-enced writer of thought-provoking historical fiction. In the summer of 2006, Ed and his wife, Susan, moved to McCormick, South Carolina where he now spends the majority of his time on writing Christian historical novels. *Family of Warriors* is his fourth book. His earlier publications are *The Stain*, *The Chaplain's Cross*, and *Revenge at Kings Mountain*, published in 2015.

CPSIA information can be obtained
at www.ICGtesting.com
Printed in the USA
FSOW01n2337060417
32733FS